"BAIL OUT, MONGOOSE! BAIL OUT!"

Less than three seconds from when he was hit Mongoose's eyes found the big yellow ejector loops at the edge of the seat. He went through the motions.

"Eject! Eject!" Shotgun's voice crackled in his ears.

He reached up and made sure his crash visor was down, helmet secure, passport punched. He yanked on the loops.

He felt a soft pop, then closed his eyes as a powerful force yanked his legs back and pushed him against the seat. The canopy blew out with a rush and the space below him exploded with a mad froth. Mongoose felt himself hurling upwards, enveloped in an icy whirlwind . . . and then he was wrapped in a dark, blank void, and then . . .

Falling . . . falling . . .

Berkley Books by James Ferro

HOGS

GOING DEEP
HOG DOWN

═**HOGS #2**═

HOG DOWN

James Ferro

BERKLEY BOOKS, NEW YORK

HOGS: HOG DOWN

A Berkley Book / published by arrangement with
the author

PRINTING HISTORY
Berkley edition / September 1999

All rights reserved.
Copyright © 1999 by Jim DeFelice.
This book may not be reproduced in whole or in part,
by mimeograph or any other means, without permission.
For information address: The Berkley Publishing Group,
a division of Penguin Putnam Inc.,
375 Hudson Street, New York, New York 10014.

The Penguin Putnam Inc. World Wide Web site address is
http://www.penguinputnam.com

ISBN: 0-425-17039-X

BERKLEY®
Berkley Books are published by The Berkley Publishing Group,
a division of Penguin Putnam Inc.,
375 Hudson Street, New York, New York 10014.
BERKLEY and the "B" logo
are trademarks belonging to Penguin Putnam Inc.

PRINTED IN THE UNITED STATES OF AMERICA

10 9 8 7 6 5 4 3 2 1

PROLOGUE

SOMEWHERE IN NORTHERN SAUDI ARABIA
21 JANUARY 1991
1600 (ALL DATES AND TIMES LOCAL)

Finally, they'd gotten a day with nearly full sun, the sort of day you'd expect in the desert. The weather had been horrible the past few days, more like Idaho than Saudi Arabia.

Private Smith rubbed his mouth, trying to chase away his late-afternoon dog breath. A few more hours and the sun would set; he'd go off duty and get some real z's— assuming Saddam didn't lob any Scuds their way tonight.

The slime.

Leaning forward against the sandbags, Private Smith stared out across the vast wasteland in the direction of the enemy, his eyes straining to separate the dust from the earth. A huge earth berm sat a few hundred yards away. It was both the border of the country and the line between boredom and insanity.

Private Jones poked him in the back good-naturedly.

"How's it going?" asked Jones.

"Not too bad," said Smith. "You get any action going on the Super Bowl yet?"

The answer to his question was drowned out by a sudden roar. Two dark monsters swept up over the nearby berm, almost on top of them. The jets were so close to the earth their wheels would have touched if their landing gear was out.

"Motherfucker!" screamed Smith, throwing himself on the ground.

The ground rattled with the sudden roar of the planes. Their noses bristled with the business ends of GAU-8/A Avenger seven-barrel rotary cannons, whose 30mm shells could chew through a concrete wall in a heartbeat. Thick wings jutted defiantly straight out from the fuselages, throwbacks to an earlier, rougher era. The planes' huge engines hung off their backs like a devil's forked tail; the rear rudders looked like legs trailing a flying witch.

The two fighter-bombers pounded over the sand like a pair of Satan's minions sent to return some escaped soul to eternal torture. Smith cowered, sure that his next address would be chiseled in granite.

"Relax," Jones told Smith as soon as the planes passed. He laughed, reached down and hauling his companion to his feet. "They're only Warthogs."

"Shit. I didn't even hear the bastards."

"Good thing they're on our side, huh?"

"Damn fug-ugly planes," said Smith, staring after them. "Uglier than the back end of a Humvee."

"Uglier than your girlfriend."

"That ain't no thing."

"Kick-ass ugly plane," said Jones. "Gonna go tank up, then go back and rip some Iraqi hide."

"I'm for that," said Smith.

PART ONE

EASY PICKINGS

1

He'd meant to read the letter from his wife earlier. In fact, he'd been meaning to read it since last night, but one thing or another got in the way. Now, sitting in the cockpit of his A-10A Warthog fighter-bomber waiting for clearance to take off, Major James "Mongoose" Johnson eyed the edge of the greenish-blue envelope, wondering if there was enough time to split it open and read it.

Probably, there was. Having just been refueled and reloaded, Mongoose and his wingman were standing at the edge of the runway, ready to launch the day's third foray behind enemy lines. But an F-16 with battle damage had been given priority to land; they were waiting for the plane to make its appearance.

Thing was, if the F-16 took too much longer, this sortie would have to be scrapped. There wasn't a heck of a lot of daylight left, and besides, the two Devil Flight Hogs had been working since before sunup nearly twelve hours ago.

He could've, should've read the letter earlier. He'd had plenty of time between the first and second missions, sitting in the refueling pit. And actually, there had been nearly a half hour after his preflight before dawn that he'd spent rechecking details that had been checked three times already.

The truth was, Major Johnson got fixated on routines as well as details; he usually read his wife's letters at night before writing to her, and missing that chance had thrown him off. It didn't feel right to read it at any other time, in any other place but his quiet bunk in Tent City.

This was the flip side of the personality that made James "Mongoose" Johnson one of the best Directors of Operations in the entire A-10A community, if not the Air Force. The positive side led him to meticulously diagram not just a planned mission route but all the alternatives. The positive side led him to take over a lot of the squadron commander's tasks, pushed him to find problems in planes that had been cleared by someone else, made him carefully evaluate not just a pilot's physical abilities but his mental state before drawing up a game plan.

The negative side made him a pain in the ass. He knew that; he was trying to be less by-the-book, bend more on the bullshit, bring out the best in people by giving them slack.

The negative side also meant that when his routine was disrupted, he tended to let things drop off the side.

Like the letter. He *could* read it now; undoubtedly it would give him a boost, as Kathy's letters always did. But somehow it didn't feel right.

Reading the letter would be like removing his helmet before goosing the throttle to take off, or undoing the straps that bound him to the ACES II ejector seat while in the middle of an invert. As tempting as it was to think about home, to savor the memory of his wife and their new baby, it was important for him to keep to his usual cockpit routine. Granted, the sortie was nothing special, easy pickings. Devil One and Two were tasked to smash the hell out of an artillery emplacement a quick drive over the border. Ride in, ride out. No big deal.

Still, it needed his full attention. The letter could wait.

A wobbling blur appeared at the edge of the afternoon sky, fumbling over the runway haze with a sizable gash in her right wing. It was the injured F-16. Johnson watched as the plane seemed to fight off a sudden burst of wind—it might actually have been a problem with the damaged control surfaces—then righted itself and skimmed into a good landing pattern.

The sleek and versatile F-16 Viper or Falcon was generally reckoned as one of the best all-around planes in the allied inventory, a hell of a dogfighter that drew second straw only to a balls-out F-15 Eagle or—and this was a heavy point of contention between the services—an F/A-18 Hornet, the versatile two-engined attack plane favored by the Navy. In contrast, Mongoose's A-10A Warthog was more a mud wrestler than a modern fighter. She was built to fly low and slow, and she looked it. Her long wings stood straight out from her pudgy fuselage, exactly the way they would have on a 1930's monoplane. The large fan-jets behind the cockpit looked as if they'd been stolen from an early 1960's airliner. Officially called the Thunderbolt II, the plane had been nicknamed the Warthog because she was twice as ugly as one.

But she was also three times as ornery. Those simple wings could hold a heavier weapons load than the average World War II bomber. The fan-jets couldn't get the Hog up to the sound barrier, but they allowed the plane to twist and turn cartwheels in the sky. Part of the A-10A's muscular frame was made of titanium; all of her important control systems were redundant and well protected. The Hog could take more lead than a target at a turkey shoot and keep on flying—a fact, not a brag; Mongoose had seen it himself. She was also incredibly easy to service, and meant to be used right in the heart of trouble. Gassing and arming her were easy enough that Army troops could do it. In fact, rumor had it that more than one Hog driver had gotten fed up with the wait over at A1 Jouf FOA the first day of the war and hopped out and refurbished his craft himself.

The tale was probably apocryphal, though Mongoose had no doubt that his wingman, Captain Tommy "Shotgun" O'Rourke, had contemplated something along those lines already.

Shotgun—the pilot of Devil Two—was exactly that kind of guy, the prototypical wingman and a born Hog driver. But he was unlike any other pilot in the entire service. His legend extended well beyond the small confines of the 535th Attack Squadron (Provisional). Shotgun could fly with one hand on the stick and the other wrapped around his coffee thermos, in manual reversion with no help muscling the controls from the hydraulics. He'd be listening to a Bruce Springsteen CD that played on the stereo in his specially modified flight getup, plunking Iraqis while microwaving a hot dog.

Actually, he didn't have a microwave in his cockpit. Yet.

The F-16 hit the runway a bit fast, wheels squealing and a wing popping up before settling down. Mongoose glanced again at his wife's letter, staring at the return address with its carefully printed blocked letters. The thin blue lines of her text were folded against themselves, showing backwards through the thin paper.

She would have used her favorite Cross pen to write the letter. It was her good-luck pen.

Maybe it wasn't anal-retentiveness about his schedule and duties that had made him put off reading the letter. Maybe it was something else, something unconscious. Bad karma or something.

Maybe he sensed bad news.

He'd devoured the other letters. Read them and read them and read them, until the words were burned into his brain.

But this one . . .

Not bad news, not a premonition, just—something weird. Like maybe it would be bad luck.

Jesus, he told himself. *You're getting like Doberman. Next thing you'll be doing is snugging your helmet exactly twelve times before getting into the cockpit.*

"Devil One?"

With a start, Mongoose realized the tower had cleared him to take off and was waiting for him to get his butt in gear.

He gave the letter a frown, then pushed it securely into his pocket.

"Sorry, honey," he told it, as if it were really his wife. "I'll get to it later. I promise."

2

Most combat pilots, especially ones facing a sortie sure to stretch several hours, stayed away from coffee hours before climbing up into their winged chariot. Most pilots would sooner bring an armed hand grenade into a cockpit than a loaded half-gallon thermos. Especially Warthog drivers. The plane lacked an autopilot, and wrestling with the piddlepack in flight was probably more hazardous than running past a dozen SA-6 installations, the fiercest Russian-made antiair missiles in Iraq.

Of course, most pilots weren't Captain Thomas "Shotgun" O'Rourke, the commander of Devil Two.

As Shotgun stowed his thermos back in its specially designed compartment in his flight suit, he considered the possibility of rigging some sort of pressurized device that would operate with a tube and spigot. This way he could sip coffee even pulling high g's. Nothing like a little caffeine to counteract the effects of all that blood rushing into, or away from, your head.

Of course, he could just go ahead and use a cup, but the ground crew tended to complain about splashes on the instruments.

Shotgun still had a few ounces of coffee in his plastic "preflight" cup, not as much as he wanted but enough to keep his hum level up for the trip north. He sipped it delicately, like a connoisseur checking out fine wine. Truth was, this Java Roast was really Chase & Sanborn from the windy side of the vineyard, but what the hell. Sacrifices had to be made in wartime.

King Khalid Military City was a forward operating area, in theory a scratch base near the front where A-10As could reload and get back into the fray as quickly as possible. But Khalid didn't look like a typical scratch base. Sure, there were Army guys running all over the place, which gave it the homey look. There was also the requisite Saudi dust, and the change in temperature could provide a very handsome fog in the early morning, exactly the sort of thing you wanted to accent sheer chaos.

But there was also an immense dome and office building complex nearby—a pit helmet and bandbox—which made the place look more civilized than Charles DeGaulle Airport, in Shotgun's humble opinion.

Now DeGaulle would be a kick-ass FOA. Those Frenchmen knew how to throw the fear of God into a pilot, the one thing they did right as far as Shotgun was concerned. Plus, as an extra bonus, you could fly under the Eiffel Tower on the way in for a landing.

The pilot gave his instruments a final check as his Hog rumbled across the tarmac. The pointy-nose F-16 had finally gotten his butt down on the airstrip in one piece. He'd obviously been shot up pretty bad, and Shotgun didn't begrudge the Viper's pilot for taking so long to land. He was, after all, working under a hardship—he wasn't driving a Hog.

Shotgun's eyes pegged the indicators on the dials over his right knee as he made sure the twin engines were running at spec. Together, they put out over eighteen thousand pounds of thrust, enough in theory to lift fifty thousand pounds of Hog off a strip faster than he could finish a Twinkie. The plane couldn't actually go all that fast—her posted top speed was 439 miles an hour in level flight at sea level, a mark Shotgun had never actually made, partly because he rarely found himself at level flight at sea level. But the Hog wasn't about speed; she was about pounding the crap out of bad guys, and that he had done, and done well. Going slow was a point of honor.

When the dials confirmed his gut feel that the power plants were pumping at shop-manual spec, Shotgun swept his eyes across the panel on the right, making sure the fuel tanks hadn't sprung a leak. Then he glanced down at the switches for the INS navigational system, marching his glance around the rest of the cockpit in a sweep that took in the radio and weapons switches and worked over to the large, globe-like horizon indicator at the top center of the dashboard before returning to the canopy. With all instruments present and accounted for, Shotgun shifted around in his seat, hunkering in the cockpit like a medieval knight getting into joust position on his horse. To his everlasting disappointment, the ACES II ejector seat could not be customized as his flight gear had been; otherwise, Shotgun might have fitted it with a gun rack and maybe a massage unit.

But then, being a Hog pilot was all about roughing it.

He reached his left hand to give his steed more throttle. The TF34 GE power plants whinnied hungrily, winding their turbofans into a snorting frenzy. The plane jumped forward, her nose sniffing the air for the smell of battle as Shotgun nudged toward the firing line. She gave the pilot a snort and a gentle shake as she flexed her muscles and strained for the sky.

He still had the coffee cup cradled in his lap. He liked to hold out as long as possible for the last sip. There was nothing like the feeling of a perfectly timed takeoff—one where gravity forced the final gulp of joe down your throat.

3

Lieutenant William Dixon shuffled through the listing of Republican Guard units the Army wanted bombed, in theory reviewing their priorities as targets, but in reality doing nothing more than providing a fifth check on someone else's math. One of Devil Squadron's most promising young pilots, Dixon was currently assigned as a "floating liaisonary aide" to the FIDO, or fighter duty officer at Black Hole. It might sound semi-impressive outside of Riyadh, but it was actually a make-work job created especially for him, a velvet-barred temporary exile cum doghouse.

Black Hole was the nickname for the command staff under Lt. General Buster Glosson in Riyadh. They prepared the daily air tasking order, essentially the daily game plan for the air war. The ATO was, in effect, Lt. General Charles A. Horner's main tool for directing the air battle, and Black Hole amounted to the right brain lobe of USCENTAF and the allied air effort against Saddam. Everything that flew higher than a grasshopper, from Marine AV-8B Harrier jump jets to U.S. Air Force F-117 stealth fighters, got its marching orders from Black Hole.

The FIDO—a rotating assignment from each squadron—

was a pilot who acted as a liaison and advisor to both the planners and the guys on the line. But as the FIDO's sidekick, Dixon wasn't here to liaison with anyone, much less give them advice. His squadron commander, Colonel Michael Knowlington, had shipped Dixon over after the lieutenant had screwed up on a mission the first day of the war and then glossed over exactly what had happened. Before being shipped out, Dixon had partly redeemed himself by shooting down an Iraqi helicopter and becoming an instant celebrity—a good thing, as far as he was concerned, or he would now be cleaning latrines somewhere in Alaska.

Dixon's contriteness after the affair had also played in his favor. Knowlington had as much as told him that if he kept his nose clean for a few days, he would rejoin Devil Squadron by the end of next week. And that meant he would find himself back in the air—the only reason to be in the Air Force at all, as far as Dixon was concerned.

So he was on more than his best behavior. Staying out of trouble wasn't all that hard actually, since his exile was more than just symbolic. The FIDO needed less than no help, and no one else at Black Hole had any place to put him. He'd been given a back desk in a back office carved from a custodian's closet in an auxiliary building some distance from the main Black Hole contingent in the Royal Saudi Air Force building. He was so far from the action scorpions didn't even bother to visit.

Which was why the knock on the outside wall literally scared the hell out of him. Dixon jerked his head up and saw the door frame filled by a six-six brusier of an Air Force officer, with round, dark black cheeks and a smiling face that seemed semi-familiar.

"Ben Greer. Remember?"

"Oh, yeah," said Dixon, rising to shake the major's hand. He and Major Greer had shared root beers together at King Fahd his first night in Saudi Arabia—neither he nor Greer drank alcohol. "How are you?"

"In one piece. How the hell are you? I hear you're a hero."

"Nah. I came around behind my lead and bam, there was

a chopper in my face. I don't know which one of us was more surprised."

"That's not the way they tell it on CNN."

"I wouldn't necessarily believe everything I heard."

"This is your reward, huh? Looks more like purgatory. I didn't even know this was an Air Force building."

"Kind of a long story."

Greer flew an MH-53J Pave Low Super Jolly Green Giant chopper, a serious piece of whirly meat specially fitted for clandestine missions behind enemy lines. Based at Fahd like the A-10As, the Pave Lows were under the direction of the Special Ops command, a special group that combined Army, Air Force, and Navy commandos. They were tasked with a variety of jobs, most importantly—at least as far as Dixon was concerned—SAR or search-and-rescue missions. They spent a lot of time in the hot and dusty regions of the war zone.

Because SAR was not specifically an Air Force operation, there was friction at the command level and a bit of grousing from some pilots, who questioned whether they would get the operational priority they needed when the shit hit the fan. Nonetheless, the crews who manned the Pave Lows were full-blooded members of the right-stuff fraternity, and Dixon felt a little awed by the much older Greer.

"Want to go grab dinner?" Greer asked.

"I'd love to but, uh, shit, this guy invited me to his house, and—"

"Coffee? Just take a minute." Greer had a strange look in his eye, as if this weren't completely a request.

"Well, sure, what the hell."

"Off-campus, so to speak."

"Off-campus?"

"I wanted to talk to you about something where we won't be disturbed. I got just the place."

"Um, okay. Let me just tell the sergeant where I'll be."

Greer gave him a you-weren't-listening squint.

"I mean, let me just tell her I'll be out for a while," said Dixon.

Ten minutes later, over some of the sweetest yet strongest

coffee Dixon had experienced outside a hangar, the major laid out a plan for a Special Ops strike of Scud sites.

It was, Dixon told him, a brilliant plan. But why, exactly, was he hearing it?

"We've been getting nowhere with the brass, and when I heard you were at Black Hole, I figured that was a message from God." Greer gave Dixon a huge, Special Ops grin— his twentieth, at least, since they had sat down.

"I don't have much influence," Dixon told him.

"You can talk to some people, right? I heard Glosson likes you."

"General Glosson? I've never even met him one on one."

"Shit, guy like you? Splashes a chopper with a Hog? They'll listen to you. Just bring it up in a meeting, offhand kinda. We can take out the Scuds. I guarantee that. We'll blow those little fuckers into so many pieces no one'll even know they were there."

"It's just I don't think I can talk anyone into it. Shouldn't you guys be working on the CINC?"

"His Cincship?" Greer gave Dixon a disrespectful grin. "Boss is working on Schwarzkopf personally. This is more a guerrilla operation me and some of the guys are drumming up."

The smile again. Then something lit in Greer's eyes, a bit too obvious to have been anything but rehearsed.

"Hey, I just thought of something," he told Dixon. "You ought to sign up for some Special Ops yourself. As an observer. I can get you in, no sweat. We can use Hog pilots."

"Go on."

"No shit. A lot of pilots are bitching about the SAR flights. You could tell them what's going on. That's how we sell it from your end, and I'll take care of it on mine. Shit, you'd be perfect. Forget SAR. You can come with us and blow up Scuds. I'll pull strings and get you on board. My colonel is an A-1 guy. Man, he loves Hogs. Loves 'em. I think he creams just thinking about them."

"I'd love to, but—"

"It's done then. My colonel'll make the call. In the meantime, make the pitch for us, okay? This is the kind of thing we've been training for."

A half hour later, Dixon found himself in his supervisor's office, repeating word for word—except for an occasional stutter—what Greer had told him.

The answer came quickly.

"No."

"I'm sorry, Major, I knew you wouldn't—"

"At ease, Dixon, relax. You're the fifth guy who made this pitch today. Special Ops is putting on a full-court press to get into the Scud game. I think they've assigned someone to work over everyone in Riyadh." The major drew back in his chair, cracking his knuckles with a full-finger spread. "I hear you're getting bored around the office."

"Who told you that?"

"Little birdie gave me a call just five minutes ago. Listen, I know the only reason you're up here is that some general somewhere wanted to make sure the press could get a look at you. Well, they have. You're chomping at the bit, aren't you?"

"I would like to get back to my squadron."

"I'll be honest with you, BJ. I know there's nothing here for you to do. I mean, besides waiting for somebody else to catch a cold. I know you've been bored. So I'm going to see what I can do about your request to ride with Special Ops as an observer. Not a bad idea actually. We need more of our guys looking over their shoulders. Keep them from getting taken over by the goddamn Green Berets. Pretty soon, our pilots are going to be driving tanks instead of helicopters."

Dixon sucked a quick, deep breath. Truth was, he hadn't exactly expected Greer to follow through on the offer, especially this fast.

Truth was, he'd be surplus material in the highly trained and capable crew that worked Special Ops.

On the other hand, this might be a kind of backhanded way of putting him back at King Fahd, where he could just walk across the tarmac to Hog Heaven and get back in the starting rotation. It might be a way of getting around all the paperwork normally involved. Knowlington knew everyone in the Air Force; hell, he'd probably set this whole rigma-role up.

"I certainly wouldn't pass up the chance to do anything, uh, anything important for the Air Force," Dixon said.

"Good. If it was up to me, SAR would be entirely an Air Force mission. Special Ops is fine, don't get me wrong, and I'm not against joint commands and all that bullshit, but—hey, this will work out. I'll get on it right away," said the major. "Listen, if anybody asks, you can handle a rifle, right?"

Dixon hesitated a moment. Since getting in trouble, he had made a solemn vow not to lie or even shade the truth.

"Absolutely, I can handle a rifle," he said finally, deciding that handling wasn't necessarily the same thing as aiming, firing, and hitting anything he happened to point it at.

4

Three quarters of the world was blue—the light, delicate blue of a woman's summer dress, inviting, scented with a fragrance that tickled and enticed.

The last quarter was hell, dirty yellow and brown, punctuated by black splotches and fingers of smoke and fire. Mongoose looked down through cockpit glass as the Hog chugged upwards, struggling to make the lofty twenty thousand feet prescribed as the "safe" altitude to cross the border. The A-10A was designed for smash-mouth, chin-in-the-mud flying. While other aircraft might consider twenty angels medium altitude, a heavily laden Hog worked up a serious sweat getting up there.

And to a Hog pilot, twenty thousand feet was just about in orbit. Hell, once the altimeter cranked over a hundred feet, most guys called for oxygen and maybe a stewardess. But the brass had ordered the planes high to put them out of range of what was left of the Iraqi air defenses; though they'd been pounded pretty well on Day One of the air war, Saddam still had a formidable array of antiaircraft guns and low-altitude missiles.

An Iraqi highway appeared in the distance as Mongoose

oriented himself. It ran in a faint, gentle arc across the earth, like the scar left from a botched suicide attempt. Somewhere along it was an artillery encampment that Mongoose and Shotgun had hit on their last run a few hours before, a five-clawed puppy paw of a site they had left mangled like a teenage girl's chewing gum. The pilot stared to the east, looking for the blotch of blackness that ought to mark it and the graves of the Iraqis who had worked the guns. There had been no resistance to speak of; the run had been quick, in and out, their bombs and missiles released from no lower than nine thousand feet, precisely as briefed. If anyone had fired at them, they hadn't noticed.

That was just fine as far as Mongoose was concerned. The medium-altitude tactics felt awkward, but you couldn't argue with the goal of getting everybody back in one piece. As the brass were fond of saying, there wasn't anything worth dying for up here.

Which wasn't to say that they wouldn't get down and dirty if the situation called for it. Mongoose pushed his back against his seat, trying to unwrench a kink that had been tightening practically since leaving King Khalid. Part of him was convinced that the Hog had knotted his muscles itself because it didn't like flying so high.

He double-checked his INS, mentally calculating that they were about ten minutes south of the quadrant in their assigned "kill box" or grid where they were to look for their target, another artillery park. Mongoose edged his eyes in that direction, his anticipation starting to build as he let the Hog nose ever so slightly into a very shallow dive. He aimed to arrive over their target at about fifteen thousand feet. The plane, happy to be on track for thicker air and sensing that she'd soon get a chance to do some snorting, gave him a happy growl, picking up speed.

Devil One and Two were each carrying a pair of Maverick B air-to-ground missiles and four Mk 20 Rockeye II cluster bombs. The Maverick B models were relatively primitive versions of the tank-busting weapon; a video camera in the nose displayed its target in a small television screen or TVM on the right side of the Hog's control panel. Once a target was designated and locked, the pilot could launch the missile and move on; the Maverick's own guidance system took over, flying its 125-pound shaped-charge warhead to the crosshairs. Newer models featured better seekers with infrared targeting and a heavier payload, but the B was still a deadly piece of meat, and only cost the Air Force about $22,000, a relative bargain—especially when compared to what it blew up.

The Mk 20 Rockeye II weapons were unguided but devastating; their bomblets spread out when dropped, a deadly hailstorm particularly suited for "softer" targets. The bombs were preset for this mission to be dropped from ten thousand feet; their need to be calibrated before taking off removed some of their flexibility and was their only real drawback.

When the Hogs were about five minutes from their target, Mongoose did one more check of his paper map and coordinates. He was just rechecking their egress route back to base when their airborne controller, Red Dog, squawked out his call sign.

"Stand by for new tasking," said the controller after running through the acknowledgment codes.

That meant, we got something juicy for you, so get your pen and paper handy.

Or in this case, your Perspex—Mongoose scrawled the heading and way markers directly onto the canopy glass with a grease pen. The nine-line brief began with an IP—an "initial point" to fly to that acted as the marker for most of the rest of the instructions.

The numbers on the glass were sending them about sixty miles further into Iraq, and well to the west, up in the direction of the Euphrates River and the better sections of the Iraqi air defense system. It was a hell of a long way to send the Warthogs, and Mongoose immediately guessed why.

He asked anyway. "What are we looking for, Red Dog?"

"Scud launchers. F-111 crew saw them on the way out. Two, possibly more. Some auxiliaries."

"Copy," said Mongoose, immediately bringing his plane to the new heading.

The Iraqis had started launching the ground-to-ground

missiles shortly after the start of the air war. Because of their range and ability to carry chemical and biological agents, Scuds had top priority as targets. So far, none had actually done much damage—but the allies' luck couldn't hold for very long.

The controller added that a Phantom Wild Weasel was being vectored into the area and would suppress any surface-to-air nasties. Like all the Weasels in the theater, the F-4 had a "beer" call sign: Rheingold One.

"The one Weasel to call when you're slamming more than one," sang Shotgun in Devil Two. "I hope this Scud launcher is the son of a bitch who woke me up last night. Man, he peed me off. I was in the middle of a wet dream."

The rest of his transmission was covered by another flight. In theory, the squadron frequency should have been reserved just for them, but the large number of allied sorties and the fog of war had a way of mangling theories.

Mongoose wasn't a particular fan of chitchat anyway, especially in this situation. If his map and memory were right, the suspected launch site was pretty close to several Iraqi SAM sites. The missiles had been hit at the beginning of the war, but that didn't necessarily mean a few weren't still there. But that was what the Weasel was for.

He took a quick glance at his instruments. Everything was at spec. His heart was well into its pre-action rumble and his throat tightened a half notch. Something inside his brain flicked a switch and the irises in his eyes widened. His situational awareness—a mental balloon of wariness around him—expanded as he gripped the stick between his knees, nudging the Hog toward the first reference marker.

His eyes turned upward as a pair of F-15 Eagles on combat air patrol screeched across the sky well ahead and above the two A-10's. The pointy-nosed fast movers had just gotten word that an Iraqi plane was scrambling from an air base nearly a hundred and fifty miles to the north. The two jets looked like a pair of famished wolves, anxious for a kill.

Mongoose put his mind and eyes back where they belonged, scouting the ground ahead. The Hog was barely making two hundred knots, moving slow because of the altitude and its bomb load.

They were just three minutes to the target coordinate when Rheingold One checked in. He was swinging in from the northwest, obviously diverted from something else. His scopes were clear.

An old soldier now, the F-4 was equipped with radar-seeking HARM missiles that homed in on antiair defenses. The missiles were extremely potent, but worked only when the radar sets were turned on—something the Iraqis had quickly learned not to do until they definitely wanted to shoot something down. The Weasel pilot sounded a little disappointed as he told Devil One things were quiet and would probably stay that way.

"Okay. Let's keep it at fifteen thousand feet," Mongoose told Shotgun. "Take a circuit and see what we can see."

"Sounds good to me."

"You see that smudge off my right wing?"

"Four-barrel ZSU, gotta be."

"Yeah, I think. Nowhere near where our missiles are supposed to be."

"I got a good view. No missiles there. Looks like some sort of APC next to it, nothing else."

"Okay, good. Let's keep our distance."

"'Less we get bored."

Mongoose held the Hog on its side so he could take a good gander at the ground, tilting his wings carefully. He told himself to break everything down, take things in pieces, and punch the buttons. This far north anything could happen. You had to go at it very deliberately.

There was no denying the adrenaline. In a certain way he almost considered this fun—not amusement-park fun, since people would or could shoot at him—but fun in the sense that it was what he was meant to do, what he was trained for and good at.

So where the hell were these things? He put his eyes back toward the antiaircraft gun he'd seen; well to the east now, its smudge had disappeared. It sat alone at the edge of the wasteland, with seemingly no reason to be agitated and too far from them to be of any immediate concern. He passed his eyes around in the other direction, noting that the desert was less stereotypical sand and dune here, more like a dirt parking lot that hadn't been used in a long time. Scrubby vegetation and even some trees poked up everywhere in the packed-dirt wasteland before giving way to the more resolute stretches of sand.

Intel had passed around various pictures of Scud sites, and both Mongoose and Shotgun had seen—and smoked— a carrier the other day. A typical launch site would arrange five or six missile erectors like fingers on a hand around a central command area. The Russian-made launchers were large trucks that looked like squashed soap pads with toilet paper tubes on them. But the Iraqis also made their own launchers from the transport trailers. From the air at this altitude they would look like long tanker trucks, dark pencils against the darker earth.

Mongoose saw nothing man-made below except the faint ribbon of a road. No trucks, no launchers, no Scuds. Definitely no base or flattened pull-off area. The Hogs were standing on the coordinates the controller had given them.

He continued the long, almost lazy figure-eight pattern around the area, gave a good scan again, and still found nothing.

"See anything?" he asked his wingmate.

"Nah. You know what the problem is? We're too high," Shotgun said. It was pretty much his answer to everything. "They could have all sorts of things camouflaged down there. We're going to have to take it down."

Mongoose reasoned that the plane that had spotted the launch site had probably been flying a lot higher than they were. "We'll hold off on that a second," he told Shotgun. "You got that highway?"

"Oh, yeah. No missin' it. Probably goes right to Saddam's house."

"Let's follow it north and see if we can find anything worth taking a look at. Launch site has to be near a road."

"Gotcha."

Thirty seconds later, Mongoose caught the glare from something small and white moving along the highway ahead. He quick-glanced at the weapons panel, but kept his stick hand solid. The white blur focused itself into a small pickup truck, too insignificant to be a target.

The road edged to the left ahead. There was a spot that seemed darker than the rest of the nearby desert; two or three shadows were at the edge, tents or something.

Good place for a bunker.

And more than that. Beyond the shadows were several rows of boxes that just had to be trucks, maybe armored personnel carriers or even light tanks.

"Shotgun, there's a wadi or something just northwest of the road where that truck is passing. Follow that and you'll see a bunker complex or some awfully funny-looking sand dunes looks like—what, maybe a mile up it. Got it?"

Before his wingmate could acknowledge, the Hog's launch warning system began shouting that Saddam's minions had just fired a surface-to-air missile in their direction.

5

For some guys, the worst time was the middle of the night. They'd lie awake in bed, sounds and shadows creeping around the periphery of their consciousness. Innocent things, or maybe not-so-innocent things, would poke at their memories, prod anxieties, fuel guilt. They'd sweat and writhe; eventually they'd get up. From there it would get worse.

Colonel Michael "Skull" Knowlington had never minded the night. Even at the worst of times, he could sleep. And if he wasn't sleeping, he was up because he had plenty to do, and having plenty to do meant he could focus on the present. That he could do; that was easy.

For him, the worst time was the middle of the day, the dead time between missions, when the paperwork was done, when he'd run out of things to check on, when he had no more calls to make or people to see. The late afternoon, with all his guys still out and everyone around him working or else off catching a quick breather—that was the worst time. That was the time when he could do nothing, and doing nothing was the worst. Doing nothing led to old memories, and old memories led to a powerful thirst.

Michael Knowlington, commander of 535th Attack Squadron (Provisional), wing commander if only on paper, decorated hero of the Vietnam War, a survivor of not just combat but the more dangerous intricacies of service politics, would do anything *not* to satisfy that thirst. He had been sober now for going on three weeks. "Skull" Knowlington needed to put one more day on that streak, just one more day.

There'd be more, a long string beyond that, but for now, just one solid, drink-free day was his goal.

For much of his Air Force career he had hated paperwork, abhorring the bureaucratic red tape and bullshit. Now he welcomed it—not because he appreciated that it was impossible to run an organization as vast and complex as the Air Force without it, but because it gave him something to focus on. But inevitably, it was over. When the colonel finished proofreading the last fitness report—something that could have waited for weeks if not months—he found his small desk completely empty. He got up, deciding to check things in the shop area, a short walk from the complex of trailers used as the squadron offices and dubbed "Hog Heaven" by the men. Besides Devil Squadron, seven A-10A units, over a hundred planes, used King Fahd as their home drome; it was also home to an assortment of helo and C-130 units, not to mention serving as a safe place to set down for anyone in the area. O'Hare on the day before Thanksgiving wasn't half as busy.

Out in the Devils' repair areas, one of Knowlington's crews was refurbishing a Hog damaged during action earlier in the week. A new starboard rudder was being fitted in place on the large double tail at the rear; the colonel stopped to watch as the wing and its new control surface were quickly made whole, a testament not only to the crew, but the men who had designed the plane for rapid repair in battle conditions.

"Colonel, can we help you, sir?" snapped off Sergeant Rebecca Rosen. She had a piece of a radar altimeter in her hand.

That or the liver of some unsuspecting airman who'd come on to her.

Officer's liver would be larger.

"I'm in good shape at the moment, Sergeant," Knowlington told her. "How about yourself?"

"Well, there was one thing, sir."

The colonel resisted the temptation to say, "How did I guess?" Instead he took a step backwards, gesturing that she should continue. One of the tricks to dealing with Rosen was to keep her away from a completely private area where she would feel at liberty to vent for hours.

She squinted, obviously debating whether to ask to speak to him in his office. The colonel, an old hand at hearing grievances real and imagined, stood hard-faced. It wasn't that he disliked dealing with true problems. Rosen, however, was a walking folder of potential disciplinary BS. She was just under five-two, with a trim and not unpleasant build, but her most distinguishing feature was the six-by-six chip on her shoulder. Knowlington's first sergeant rated her among the best technicians in the Air Force, an expert on the Hog's avionics, and a tireless worker. He also had her pegged as the top problem magnet in the squadron, a judgment Knowlington couldn't argue with.

"The other afternoon," she said. "Captain Meyer, sir, well he, uh—"

"Okay, now tell me. Meyer is who?" Knowlington asked.

Rosen stopped, her eyes receding into their sockets as she realized she had miscalculated. The E-5 had obviously expected Meyer to complain about something she'd done; now that Rosen realized he hadn't, she beat a slippery retreat. The squirm on her face was almost worth the pain she'd cause Knowlington the next time. "Um, never mind, sir. I have to get this installed pretty much right away."

"Any time, Sergeant," said Knowlington cheerfully.

He distributed a few other nods, making sure the crewmen knew he was there but trying at the same time not to bother them. A good part of his job as commander was to be a cheerleader, as much as possible applauding the men—and now women—coming up with incentives to keep the team together and moving in the right direction, but trusting his subordinates as much as possible to do their jobs. Over the past few years he'd found it less and less necessary to be a scumbag; either the Air Force was getting better, or he was.

A Navy A-6 Intruder touched down on the runway with a loud screech. Knowlington stepped forward to watch as the muscled gray swallow taxied. The first time he'd seen one he'd been at Da Nang, diverted for an emergency landing after flying a bit too close to a triple-A battery in his Thud. He was in good enough shape to circle the field while the Navy pilot, low on fuel, made his own pit stop. The plane had suffered an unexplained electronics failure, a common failure of planes of the era, Intruders especially.

They had beers later. The Navy guy, a lieutenant with two tours under his belt, bemoaned the fact that he would take a hell of a ribbing when he got back to the carrier; real pilots brought their planes back to their ship, no matter what.

Later, on their third or fourth beer, Knowlington saw the glance. It was the first time he'd truly seen fear in a pilot's eye. In retrospect, he realized that he'd seen other signs before, but not recognized them, didn't know what they meant: the furtive glance at your hands, the slight hesitation before speaking, the quick order of another drink, the urge to talk too much. It wasn't fear so much as being afraid of fear; it was doubting yourself, and that was what killed you.

He heard later the guy had been shot down on his very next mission. MIA.

Knowlington tired to move his mind off the past, think of something else as the Intruder disappeared down the runway. Hell of a thing, trying to land on a carrier. Skull had never had the pleasure, and he counted himself lucky. Landing on a dime was one thing; landing on something that rolled beneath you was quite another.

Another thing to make you doubt yourself, squinting for the ball in the dark when you were just about out of gas and probably had to take a leak besides.

Intruders were supposed to be pretty stable bombers, muscular workhorses that carried a ton-load of bombs — fifteen thousand to sixteen thousand pounds — off a carrier without breaking a sweat.

Thuds were champion haulers themselves. The notched-wing fighter-bombers had been designed to hump nukes at breakneck speed over enemy lines and get the pilot back in one unradiated piece. Skull had carried some dummy nukes very early in his career, but what he'd used the F-105 for was dropping sticks on the North Vietnamese. He'd been pretty damn good at it too.

Carrying a nuke. Now there was a pucker-ass job, if you stopped to think about what you were doing. Some of the real old-timers talked about jets where they knew they'd never get away from the blast. Who was it—Schroeder, maybe?—who'd laughed about the F-84 hanging his butt over Cuba three days in a row?

No, that was a different story. They had a tendency to blur together.

Damn, he wanted a drink.

His heart started pounding. He was in the Thud, Ol' Horse, plane one, stone ages. Smell of raw kerosene and something that reminded him of a dentist's office thick in his nose. Muscling the stick after dropping his load. Tail-end Charlie and he'd lost the rest of the flight. Just like the nugget he was.

Nothing to panic about. Knowlington brought the plane around to his course, climbing, and then something happened, something made him crane his neck back. Maybe it was training or luck or intuition or just random chance, but as the young pilot pitched his eyes toward the rear quarter of his plane, he saw the double dagger of a MiG-17 coming up to get him.

They were tough little bastards, in theory obsolete but in reality more than competent dogfighters. They got you in a furball and you could easily get your throat slit. The eggheads could pretend the F-105 had them outclassed, but experience said otherwise. Had Knowlington not realized the bastard was on him, he would have been nailed in thirty seconds.

But he saw him. And instead of opening the engine gates and running like hell—his briefed routine, his orders, the prudent thing to do, what he absolutely would have done in ninety-nine out of one hundred other chances—Knowlington tucked his wing, pushing the stick as he began a ballet maneuver that suckered the MiG into following into a dive-and-scissors roll. He saw it all in his head a split second before it happened, the second of danger as the enemy sighted him, the spin around instead of breaking off, behind the enemy now, the 20mm M61A1 cannon rotating slowly at first, then gaining momentum as he caught the MiG just behind his right wing, stayed with him as the plane jinked, stayed with him until he realized the commie bastard was out of it, saw the wing breaking off even as he fought his own stick to level out, and now he was getting the hell away. Straight on course for home.

It turned out another F-105 pilot had seen the whole thing, raved like hell, and Knowlington had earned the first of his long series of "good" nicknames, "Killer Kid," and notched an improbable air-to-air victory in a plane not known as much of a dogfighter. His victory was due as much to surprise and probably inexperience on the MiG pilot's part as his own skill, but that was the sort of thing that got glossed over in the first rush of victory, and in any event he'd had plenty of chances later to show it wasn't just luck that kept his wings in the air.

So long ago now, though the surprise in his chest when he realized he'd nailed that son of a bitch still felt fresh.

More than twenty years. Shit, twenty-five. He should be long since retired.

Or made a general, though everyone knew why that hadn't happened.

Skull blinked his eyes and turned away from the runway, hoping to wipe his mind clear. Replaying old glories was something you did when you were sitting down for dinner at the old-age home.

Or when you were drinking. He headed back toward his office. Maybe he'd reread the Devils' frag, the portion of the air tasking order that pertained to them. The next day's to-do list had ten of the squadron's twelve planes committed to battle. It was a tight schedule, with one left in the repair shop and only one other as a spare. Even so, if the crew got the damaged plane back together in time, the backups might be tasked for their own mission.

Knowlington was dying to lead a mission himself. He'd been told not to, and there were good reasons for him to follow orders—starting with the fact that they were orders—but still. What good was a squadron commander who didn't fly?

He put his head down, pushing the question and its inevitable answer from his mind as he walked back toward his office.

He was a few steps from the door to Hog Heaven when he was caught by the bear-like voice of Chief Master Sergeant Allen Clyston, his "capo di capo" who not only headed the squadron's enlisted contingent, but oversaw the squadron's maintenance efforts personally, arranged for all manner of off-line items to appear with paperwork signed (or lost), and knew more than the World Book Encyclopedia on any subject anyone could quiz him on.

In short, a typical first sergeant.

"There you are, Colonel," said the sergeant in his most respectful public voice. Clyston's grin, though, betrayed the fact that he had known Knowlington well before he'd achieved that rank. He had, in fact, been a member of the crew that took care of the Thunderchief Knowlington had just been thinking about.

The sergeant's memory of the plane would undoubtedly be a great deal different than the colonel's. The Thunderchiefs were notoriously difficult to maintain.

"What's up, Allen?"

"Got a little bit of a hitch. Need a check pilot, and Captain Rogers is down with that flu or whatever the hell he's got. Still puking his guts out."

"Three's back together?"

"My guys got it buffed and shined, Colonel. Shit, you give them any more time and they're going to put a sunroof in."

"I'll take it up," snapped Knowlington.

"Sir?"

The "sir"—with its attached tone of surprise—hurt. Knowlington endeavored to turn it into a joke. "Afraid I'm going to break your plane?"

"No, sir, Colonel. Not at all. I just thought maybe you'd borrow somebody from one of the other units."

Though he commanded the squadron, Knowlington had come to his post through a roundabout series of events, and actually had barely a hundred hours in the A-10 cockpit, by far the lowest of the squadron's pilots. The inspection flight called for a prescribed set of maneuvers designed to stress its systems in different regimes; it was far from a picnic, and ordinarily handled by a functional test pilot, someone who had considerable experience with the plane.

Still, it was no reason for the concern evident on his sergeant's face.

"You're thinking I can't do a milk run?"

"No way, sir. You'll do fine."

"Good. When do you need me?"

"As soon as you can, Colonel."

"Good. I'll be right over."

Clyston held eye contact for just a second longer than necessary. Knowlington gave his old crew chief a sharp punch to the shoulder. "Meet you out back, Sergeant," he said, heading away before his old friend could decide what words ought to go with that look.

6

In normal times, Lieutenant Colonel Fred Parsons flew a commercial 747 for American Airlines. The big Boeing was a handsome plane, predictable, steady, and recently up-graded with every bell and whistle the Seattle wizards could stuff into the cockpit. She was everything the FAA and a travel agent could want in an airliner.

Which mean she was boring as hell.

The G model F-4 Phantom he was hot-sticking had more miles on her than a fleet of Greyhound buses. Smoke poured out of her tail thicker than a wet barbecue, making her easy to spot at a distance. In full-afterburner go-for-it mode she could top the sound barrier, but the Vietnam-era mainstay couldn't come close to matching the top end of an Eagle or even the Grumman Tomcat, her Navy successor. This particular plane also had a tendency to drag her left wing—not so much that the maintenance crew could figure out what the hell it was, but enough so the pilot felt it on a hard-butt turn.

He loved it.

Never very good as a twisty-turny hot rod, the Phantom hailed from an era when designers first realized missiles and beyond-visual-range tactics were the way to go in a dog-fight—and got so excited about the future that they forgot about the present. Her real value was as a sled for every imaginable weapon and fantasy the Air Force and Navy could load under her wings. The Phantom was still flying now, nearly forty years after being conceived, because the two-seater could accommodate all manner of equipment without completely compromising performance. Something over fifty radar antennas were currently feeding data to Parsons' backseat wizard, who in the great tradition of weapons officers or backseaters went by the name of "Bear." The Phantom could carry nearly her weight in arms and fuel—and at 29,000 pounds soaking wet, that was a very full load of groceries. The fact that she had a backseat allowed Parsons to concentrate on flying while Bear studied the dials and maybe the latest copy of *Playboy*.

Equipped with extra fuel tanks, the Phantom could also stay aloft for an incredibly long time, an asset that Parsons was putting to good use at the moment, just entering his third hour in Indian country. He and another Weasel had started the afternoon with a bombing package, looking to suppress integrated SAM defenses deep in Iraq. The other Weasel had launched a pair of missiles at one of the sites, but otherwise the mission had been so quiet Parsons had gladly brushed aside his fatigue when the request came to assist the Hogs on their Scud-hunting gig.

"I'm beginning to think they're out," said Bear, whose dog tags identified him as Captain Harvey Jackson, another member of the Air National Guard and a high school English teacher in what he called the real world. Intel suspected that at least one battery of SA-2's and another of SA-6's were still breathing below. "If they're not coming up for those Hogs, they're never coming up," Bear predicted. "They should be able to see them. I say we got three minutes to worry about, then it's downhill. I hope these assholes try something—I want that SA-6."

"Me too. But not if it nails our little buddies."

"Hey, those Hogs are tough bastards. I bet you could put a missile through each wing and they'd still come home—after they made their bomb run."

"Probably been done."

"Don't worry, Fred. I'm not letting them get hit."

In some of the early-model Phantoms, the backseater could look past his control panel and see the pilot; in fact, it was possible to pass notes back and forth and even lean forward or backward for an ataboy. In the Gs, though, the two crewmen were separated by an "iron wall"—actually a wall of aluminum and glass, electronics, wires and gauges, but it might just as well be iron as far as Bear in his cave was concerned. Fly with the same guy long enough, though—or through enough shit—and the distance disappeared. His thoughts became your thoughts; the back-and-forth chatter became a kind of binary code plugging into your head.

"I'm going to take us further north near that SA-6," Parsons told Bear. "I have a feeling they're down there and waiting."

"Hang loose, Colonel."

It wasn't the words but the tone that told the pilot his backseater had a tingling. The APR-47 radar attack and warning receiver sniffed out a quick hit as Parsons' grip on the stick tightened.

"Oh, yeah," Bear said. "He's turning it on and off. Just a two-second burst. I have him. SA-2. Hasn't launched yet. Okay, okay."

"Roger that. Scope's clear except for Squeaky," answered Parsons. "Putting him on beam."

"Still looking for the SA-6."

"I have ten miles to target. That SA-2 battery's going to launch any second. You ready to fire?"

"PPI has it," said the pitter, referring to the Plan Position Indicator, which displayed enemy threats in relation to the Weasel. "I'm handing off."

It took a bare second for the Phantom's computer to send the targeting information to the HARM AGM-88 missile under her wing. The antiradiation missile took in the numbers, crunched them to fit, and blipped the light on Bear's panel, telling him it was ready to talk turkey with the Iraqis.

"Got a light."

"Launch."

"Missile away."

"They've launched!" Parsons saw the ground flash and blew hard into his mask. The SA-2 had been in action since the Vietnam War; it had a small bag of tricks, and to a plane as fast and as high as Rheingold One, it did not pose much of a threat. Still, he had to be careful. He was just about to push the Phantom into a roll when his backseater shouted into the com set.

"Son of a bitch—there's two batteries. Hold it—there's our SA-6. Colonel, go to twenty-five-mile scope."

"Roger that. We got a telephone pole headed in the other direction. Get the six first. How far is it?"

"Fifteen miles. In two, start your turn to the left. We'll take a beam shot, then go back for the twos."

"Shit—more launches. The twos. I thought these motherfuckers were hit Day One. It looks like Cape Canaveral down there."

Parsons tightened his grip on the control stick. The SA-6's, persistent missiles immune to the ECM pods used by many USAF planes in theater, had top priority.

The Hogs were on their own against the SA-2's.

7

Somewhere at the edge of his consciousness, the radar warning receiver was lit up like a Christmas tree, telling Mongoose that the missile was coming at him from the northeast. By the time the information fully registered, the pilot had already begun turning the plane to "beam" the missile's radar-guidance system—pulling the Hog ninety degrees to the radar to defeat its pulse-doppler signals.

"Missile in the air," said Shotgun, his voice cold and crisp in Mongoose's helmet.

When his first maneuver and the chaff failed to shake the missile, Mongoose rolled the Hog, tucking his right wing to the earth as his eyes hunted the sky for the enemy bullet. Gravity crashed into his face and side, Newton's laws of motion making him work for a living. His fingers tightened on the control stick as he felt the Hog tug a bit. The Mavericks and Rockeyes were still tied to his wings, but the plane wasn't complaining so much as letting him know it could still do its job once this diversion was over.

First he had to get clear. He poked his nose back, still coming down, but the last thing he wanted to do was fly right into the son of a bitch.

But it was fine. Around it was okay. Away from it was better.

Shotgun yelped something else. The words rushed by incomprehensibly.

Mongoose looked in the direction the warning unit advised, but saw nothing. The edge of his helmet slammed against his neck as he jerked his head around; the sting crept down his back like a pack of night crawlers.

The Weasel pilot barked something at him, another break most likely.

More missiles. His warning unit had them.

One problem at a time.

He sucked air hard twice before his eyes found the thick telephone pole pushing toward him. It looked more like a tree trunk propelled by a tornado than a missile, more blunted than streamlined. Mongoose caught a good glimpse of its nose as he pushed the Hog down, trading altitude for energy and speed. He was lucky; he could already tell from the trajectory that the missile would miss him. It was too big to come back to his course. Too big, too fat, too ugly, too old, even for a slow mover like the Hog.

He was clear; none of the other missiles had locked on him.

He had a good view of one of them. Big bastard, but kind of a wimp—didn't even have the guts to spin back in his direction and keep the fight going.

Then he realized the missile was going after Shotgun, whose big green shadow passed through a low cloud a depressingly short distance from the thirsty, blunt nose of the SA-2.

8

Shotgun fired another round of chaff and kicked a couple of flares out the back for good measure. He could feel the missile starting to breathe in gulps, like a tiger closing in for the kill.

"Screw yourself," he told it, bending the nose of the Hog as he jackknifed the airplane toward the ground. He rolled and caught sight of the missile closer than he'd suspected, so close, in fact, that he knew he'd almost blown it big time.

He saw the wobble and then the shock wave that consumed the SA-2's long shaft as the warhead exploded. He saw that before he felt it, before he hunked his shoulders up and reflexively ducked his head, steadying the stick and telling the Hog not to worry. Energy and shrapnel rushed toward him; he swept his plane to the left, riding some of the wave but rocking like all hell, knowing they were going to make it okay. He squeezed the A-10 close to him, swaying with her like a teenager at the prom, whisking her off to a quiet corner of the dance floor where he could feel beneath her bra without the chaperons taking notes.

Of course, that was exactly the sort of thing that got him

kicked out, that and the beer cans in his tux, but what the hell.

His plane stable again, the pilot keyed his mike, not for Mongoose or Rheingold, but for the Iraqi who'd launched the missile:

"Missed, Saddam. Kind of a sissy explosion, you ask me."

Mongoose replied, but Shotgun didn't have time to explain, spotting a fresh trio of pencils silhouetted against the ground, rising off his right wing just as he began pushing his nose back toward the few scattered clouds in the sky.

"More missiles," he called. He squeezed his chaff button and began a new jinking routine.

All this maneuvering was starting to work up a good sweat, the kind of thing Gatorade was invented for.

Problem was, he hadn't packed any. Shotgun pitched the Hog back for the ground. This time he was putting the plane down so low not even a gopher could follow it.

All three missiles were coming for *his* butt, not his commander's. Which was what he got for making smart-ass remarks over the radio.

One of the SA-2's inexplicably disappeared. The other two kept coming. Shotgun leaned forward in his seat as the radar warning receiver started to get frantic. He was out of tinsel, and didn't have all that much sky left in front of him either.

SA-2's ought to get lost in the ground effects, their guidance system confused by the natural shadows and echoes thrown up by the earth.

Nope. They were coming for him big time.

The Hog didn't like this. She had her head down and was running for all she was worth, screaming as she broke below two thousand feet.

She didn't like to run away. She wanted to turn around and nail the missile in the teeth with a few rounds from her gun.

Shotgun held on, skimming the ground at five hundred, four hundred, two hundred feet. By all rights he should have been clear by now—that or bagged—but he could feel he wasn't. As he jinked, the shadow of one of the missiles poked into the far corner of his vision, dark and ugly. Stinking Saddam must have loaded this one up personally and fueled her with his piss, because the bitch was staying with him.

The missile was now in terminal-intercept phase—its onboard guidance system had locked on the Hog. It didn't have to hit him; it just had to get close. There was no question of outrunning the missile in the much slower airplane, and Shotgun didn't seem to be lucky enough to outlast it.

No way the damn missile should still be on him. At two hundred feet?

Maybe it smelled his Twinkies.

He yanked the Hog back, pushing, shoving, straining, standing the sucker on her tail as its nose spat right in the missile's face before he shoved back toward the dirt in almost the opposite direction.

It was like flashing a mirror in front of a charging bull and then diving down a manhole. The SA-2 twisted to follow the last echo of its radar, shuddering as its momentum carried it beyond the Hog.

It exploded with an angry tear, but by then Shotgun had revved the engines higher than an Indy race car, flinging himself away from the last SA-2, which had been flying roughly parallel and maybe a hundred yards behind the first. He was so low he could have landed, and the explosion rattled the American plane bad, pushing it down and yanking its tail sideways so violently that at first the pilot thought he'd been hit.

By the time he managed to steady the plane and dance his eyes through the gauges to confirm he was still in one piece, Shotgun was heading for a small observation post on a hill that stood over the desert like a crow's nest. He had maybe three inches of clearance over the roof and had he lowered his landing gear he could have wrecked it.

Shotgun would have left the post alone and started tacking north to hook up with his lead if it weren't for the fact that the Iraqis manning the post decided to protest his low flight by firing every weapon they could find at him. Fortunately, they had nothing more formidable than AK-

47's, and possibly the newer AK-74's, which had almost no recoil, a really good bark when you pulled the trigger, and a bullet that squished up good like a dumdum.

Deadly against a person at a few hundred yards, but useless against a Hog.

Still, it was the thought that counted. Hunkering in his titanium bathtub, Shotgun brought the plane around in a quick, tight bank. No one fired at a Hog without paying for it. He dialed up his cannon, steadied his hand, and let loose with a stream of high-explosive and depleted uranium that turned the position into a dervish of sand and burnt flesh.

Past the outpost, he gunned the throttle and nosed northwards, looking for Mongoose.

As he did, he reached inside his flight suit and hit the replay on his CD unit until he could hear the beginning of "Born in the USA." Something about that song brought out the best in an airplane, no shit.

9

Whoever was working the Iraqi SA-6 missile battery was either very good or very cautious, or both. Since the brief blip that alerted Bear to his presence, the intercept radar had been completely silent.

It didn't matter, though—the Weasel Police had his number. Parsons took a half second to make sure the SA-2's weren't a threat, and then closed for the kill.

The Phantom wasn't completely immune to the SA-6. The missile had a range of approximately fifteen kilometers, and its control radar used two different bands and could acquire multiple targets. The SA-6 itself could out-maneuver a fighter, and contained its own semiactive radar; once fired, it stood a better than average chance of hitting its target even with countermeasures going full tilt.

"Turning," called Parsons, pulling the Phantom in a sharp bank directly toward the missile's now-silent radar.

"Two is back up. Okay, here's our six again. We're going to nail the bastard. Okay. Hand off."

Bear was busier than a one-armed paper hanger behind the iron wall separating the two men. The computer took the target information on the SA-6 and gave it to the HARM missile's onboard guidance system; the big AGM-88 took the info, hiccuped, then thundered away. Immediately Bear dialed in one of the two SA-2 radar sites the plane had detected.

"Got the light," he told Parsons.

"Fire!"

"Away."

The thud of the rocket igniting beneath the gull-shaped wings felt reassuring. Parsons had already started a jink to keep his butt clean, planning on spinning back to pull the Phantom in the direction of the last SA-2 battery. He could see ground fire from antiaircraft cannons, too far off to bother anyone. One of the A-10As was cutting paper dolls out of sky in the distance, evading a SAM.

"Keep your turn coming," Bear told him. "I have one more. He's up. He's dotted." The backseater's slang referred to the icons on his screen that said the enemy radar had been located and targeted by the Phantom's gear.

"Handing off," Bear said, giving the target information to the missile so it could attack while he concentrated on finding more threats.

"Optical launches on those twos," warned the pilot.

"Ready light!"

"Fire."

"Away. Shit—we got that six. Mama! Secondaries. There we go! Got the trailer on the two! Whole damn thing's burning like all hell. Oh, yeah, baby! Kick ass!"

The HARM's warhead was designed to explode large, nasty shards of tungsten into the control facility of the missile's radar. By doing that, the HARM wiped out the valuable electronics gear, rendering the battery useless. It was a more effective way of destroying a threat than blowing a hole in a radar dish, which could be easily repaired.

It also generally meant you got the men working the missile. The good ones were harder to replace than the gear they worked.

Parsons caught a glimpse of the damage through the top of the canopy as he rolled the Phantom and began letting off chaff. One of the SA-2's that had been fired before the site was hit was now headed in their direction.

"Telephone pole's gunning for us," the pilot told his backseater. A way of apologizing for the six-and-a-half g's he pulled as he yanked the F-4 around to confuse the missile's guidance system. The force of the maneuver squeezed his mouth and made his words sound strange, even to him. As he recovered, he juiced the throttle, accelerating to put a good hunk of real estate between the Phantom and the Iraqi missile. But the missile, fired without proper targeting to begin with, had already fallen away.

"Hogs are still with us," reported the backseater.

"Devil Flight, this is Rheingold One. Sorry for the excitement," Parsons told the A-10's.

"No problem," snapped Devil One. "We like things hot."

The colonel did a quick check of his systems, made sure he hadn't caught something in the nether reaches of the plane. His fuel was still pretty good, but they'd fired all their radiation missiles; time to call it a day.

"How you doing in your cave back there, Bear?"

"'Bout ready to take a nap," said the pitter.

"Miles to go before you sleep," said the pilot.

"Hey, I'm the English teacher. When did you study Frost anyway?"

"Haven't you heard? Mandatory training for all airline pilots."

"I'll be impressed when you quote Whitman."

"'Flood tide below me, I see you face to face,'" said Parsons, reciting the beginning of "Crossing Brooklyn Ferry."

It was the only part of the poem, or Whitman for that matter, that he knew, but it was good enough to elicit a snort of surprised approval from Bear.

10

The plane the A-10A reminded Knowlington of wasn't the Thud, which, after all, was a straight-line in-and-out mover, but the Spad—the propeller-driven A-1 Skyraider, a Navy plane adopted by the Air Force for close-in ground-support work. Drawn up at the tail end of World War II as a torpedo bomber, the Spad was a throwback to an era when sticking really meant sticking.

Knowlington had never actually been assigned to an A-1—he'd been a pointy-nose, fast-mover jock from day one—but he'd wormed his way into the Spad's cockpit a few times to satisfy his curiosity. He'd even once volunteered for a combat mission, though he was probably lucky he'd been turned down. He was flying Phantoms by then, and if a Viet Cong gunner hadn't gotten him, the shock to his system would have.

Still, the A-1 was a hell of a plane, all stick and rudder, able to eat bullets with the best of them. She had her quirks—Skull always had a bit of trouble with the armament panel; it was right above his knee but he had a bad angle while flying. No matter; the plane felt substantial around you, like a big old Mercedes. You had a fairly good flying position high up top, unlike the Phantoms, and especially the early Thuds, where you were in a cave. And she did what she was told. Think left and you moved left. She could stand just about stock-still if you wanted, stand there and pound the bejezuz out of what you were looking at.

The Hog was like that, only a bit faster.

Well, maybe not faster, come to think about it.

Skull thought right bank and the Hog went right bank. He pulled the stick back and she corrected, her forked tail snapping into place like a slot car coming out of a turn. He pulled a few more turns, each one a little sharper, making sure the control surfaces were still in place and working well.

Even though he'd flown the Hog back in the States as much as he could, Knowlington had been awkward as hell his first few flights over here, muscling the plane through her paces, hitting his marks mechanically. It wasn't physical, it was mental—like he was thinking about flying, or maybe worrying about what some of his more senior pilots must be thinking: old man in a plane, old washed-up hack shuffled into the wrong command.

No one said that, of course, but he could read it. More than one Centcom staffer just about told him he was washed up, though the generals were much more tactful—most of them, after all, had been his friends for a long time. Inside the squadron, there was plenty of resistance, even from Major Johnson, maybe especially from him. Johnson felt with some justification that he could lead the squadron, and probably resented being number two behind a guy who'd hardly even flown the plane. A-10 drivers were a special fraternity among combat pilots; their mission and plane were different than anyone else's, and they tended to be different too.

Good pilots definitely, but with maybe the tiniest of chips on their shoulders about it.

A few realized that Knowlington had helped save the Hogs and possibly their jobs from the scrap yard, volunteering when he got word through the back channels that the CINC himself wanted more Hogs in Saudi Arabia for the ground war. They were grateful, but even *they* thought he was too far removed from "real" flying to lead them into battle.

Nobody mentioned his drinking. No one ever had.

The gray-haired colonel in him agreed that he ought to stand aside for the younger men when it came to flying missions; most of them were better Hog pilots than he'd ever be. But this afternoon he felt something ease into place as he snapped himself into the A-10A's ejector seat, something familiar; as he pushed the nose up and started to climb toward ten thousand feet, Colonel Michael "Skull" Knowlington lost track of the line that separated himself from the plane. Some awkwardness lingered. He kept expecting more in the HUD, and maybe a better view out of the side of the canopy; his eyes tripped when they felt for the fuel gauge. But he knew this plane the way he knew the others; after so many years of estrangement, the sky had welcomed him back.

No reason I shouldn't go north, he told himself. As long as I'm not a liability, it's where I belong.

Except that the generals above him wouldn't like it too much. As long as he didn't screw up, they wouldn't court-martial him over it, of course, but they could force him to retire.

Then his string of non-drinking days would surely end.

Knowlington pushed the Hog through a series of twists and turns, gradually increasing the pressures against the control surfaces. He had written down a cheat sheet with all the maneuvers, just to make sure he didn't miss any. But he didn't even have to glance at it. His hands were slower, true, and his eyes—damn, his eyes weren't the telescopes they'd once been. But his head was still there; that was as sharp, sharper than ever.

Your head could also be a liability. Memories were like bullets in your wing. One slipped into his brain now as he pulled the Hog into a steep dive. He tried to work it away, ignore it, even closed his eyes, but it came back, hard and fresh.

He was in a Phantom. They had just pulled out of a dive every bit as steep, bombing a bridge near the Laos border.

Knowlington recovered and started the long run home. His wingman called out a SAM launch.

Soviet telephone poles coming for them. The SA-2 was relatively new then, very formidable. But he had encountered them a few times before; so had his wingman. He jinked the missile onto his beam, pulled a few g's, and let the engine roar. Nothing to it.

But his wingman couldn't break free. Somehow, some way, Captain Harold "Crush" Orango had taken a SAM right in the tail. Skull's backseater saw the hit, and saw, or thought he saw, two ejections and chutes. By the time Skull recovered from his evasive maneuvers and made sure his six was clean, they had lost track of the stricken Phantom's crew. Skull cranked back, unable to find the parachutes in the low-lying clouds or draped in the jungle below. They found the wrecked Phantom soon enough—the sucker kicked up more smoke than a flaming oil tanker—but the pilot and weapons officer were nowhere to be found.

Skull keyed his mike and called in the crash. At the same time, he greased his Phantom down to treetop level, looking for his buddy in the thick canopy of trees. He'd flown with Crush on something like twenty missions; he wasn't about to lose him.

Hell damn, he'd have to start paying for his own drinks.

There was no ground beacon, no signal from the pilot's emergency radio. They were over Laos a few miles, not the best area to be. For all Skull cared he could have been pulling circuits over the Kremlin. He crisscrossed twice, low and slow, he and his backseater taking turns peering out the side, looking in vain for a pucker of nylon or a flash from a signal mirror.

He spotted a village-sized clearing at the edge of the canopy just to the east, probably straddling the border with North Vietnam, though he wasn't about to get out a map and check. Holding the F-4 about as slow as it would go, he eased toward it. The clearing was a perfect place for a chopper to land; with luck Crush would be hiding nearby.

Red and brown rocks rose from the jungle to his left as he approached. There was a long rift in the ground, a mountain ridge heaved up by some ancient geological pressures that

had dented the South Asian peninsula. He passed the
clearing.

"See anything?" his backseater asked.

They called him Little Bear. Not exactly original, but he
claimed to be part Cherokee.

Might've been bull.

"Negative. I'm trying another sweep."

"Copy."

Skull brought the Phantom back around, her engines
whining. Fuel burn was light. Flaps felt a bit sluggish for
some reason. He was at five hundred feet, slipping toward
three hundred as he made the pass, lower than the top of the
nearby ridge.

Nothing. And nothing again on the third run. He brought
the plane up. This much flying over any one spot in
Southeast Asia was extremely dangerous, especially at low
altitude.

But where was Crush? On the other side of the ridge? He
took the Phantom around, still craning his head toward the
ground for a sign of something.

"I'm going to run along that escarpment a way," he told
Little Bear.

"Shit—a mirror. Right wing. See it?"

His backseater leaned forward past his equipment to poke
him in the back and make sure he had his attention. Skull
looked over his shoulder out the F-4's canopy, but couldn't
see the light, couldn't see anything but the infinite variations
of green below.

"Where?" he asked.

"Back there. It was something."

"Yeah, hang on. I'll go back."

He could barely contain himself or the Phantom as he
pulled around for a better look. He put his wings almost on
the trees, holding the jet barely above stall speed, begging
the mirror to catch a fresh glint of the strong, overhead sun.

He got a nose full of cannon fire as a reward. What
seemed like a hundred thousand 23mm antiaircraft guns
opened up on him from the ridge.

There was a disconnect for a second, a short between his
brain and his body. Knowlington's hand threw the throttle to

afterburner, or maybe beyond; the rest of him reacted to push the plane into a line over the ridge and out of fire. None of this registered in his brain. All the pilot saw was black lead headed straight at him from all directions, red muzzles burning into his eyes.

Breaking off was the prudent thing to do, the thing any commander would have insisted he do, the thing that was right. He did it as soon as his limbs began taking instructions from his brain again.

It felt very, very wrong.

They were back at twenty thousand feet, still climbing and halfway to Burma, before his backseater's voice pulled him back to the plane.

"Throttle stuck," he said lamely. He began pulling the Phantom back, but he was spooked. They were now low on fuel, so low that he couldn't have made another pass even if he wanted to. He radioed a warning about the antiair and headed back to home base in Thailand.

That was when the real drinking started.

No one ever found Crush or his backseater. They weren't among the prisoners released at the end of the war, nor did their names show up among the dead, either in the North or interred in Laos. Their names were on the Wall; Skull had traced his finger over them himself.

Officially, the Air Force decided that the two men had gone down with the plane; unofficially, Knowlington knew that was a bunch of bull, since then the Vietnamese would have recovered the bodies. The reds had definitely found the plane; they had released propaganda photos of it as part of a campaign to prove that America had no respect for Laos's borders.

As if the scumbags did themselves.

Despite the fact that he'd driven through a cloud of flak, Skull's Phantom didn't have a nick on it when he landed. A lot of guys interpreted that as one more sign of his incredible luck. Even Little Bear was amazed.

Knowlington saw it as confirmation that he had chickened out, and was a coward at heart.

All the recognition, all the medals that had come before

that flight—and certainly those that came later—couldn't counterbalance those dark five minutes on that sortie.

He never talked about it with Little Bear. In fact, he started avoiding his backseater, worried that he might want to talk about the mission, about his chickening out. The weapons officer would have known the throttle sticking was a bunch of bull. He would have felt the second of indecision. He would have known they should have toughed it out despite the gunfire—prudence be damned.

"Devil Twelve, Devil Twelve, this is Fahd Control. Colonel, how are you reading me?"

"Twelve. Go ahead, Control."

"Sir, we need to move you around a bit."

Snapped back to the present, Knowlington did a quick check of his instruments before responding. The plane was flying at spec and had passed all her tests; no need to keep it up any longer than necessary. Tightening his grip on the stick, the colonel pushed a long breath of air out of his lungs into his face mask, reminding himself to stay in the present, to work on just today. He told the controller that what he'd really like to do was land.

"Ah, Miller time, is it?"

"Something like that," he told the kid.

Spinning back to take his slot in the landing pattern, Skull admired the way the Hog picked her tail up and put her nose right where he wanted; he tried hard not to think of anything else.

11

Mongoose heard Shotgun and had his bearing, but still couldn't see him. He continued climbing, spotting the highway they'd been flying along earlier but still without his wingman in view. Finally he caught the plane in the distance, well lower than he thought it would be.

He keyed the mike and asked Shotgun if he was all right.

"Yeah, I told you I'm fine. Iraqis couldn't hit a zeppelin."

Damned if Shotgun didn't sound like he was munching on something. And did he have his music cranked?

"Can you see me?" Mongoose asked.

"Yeah. Gonna take me a minute."

"We'll come east and follow that highway again. You see it?"

Their little adventure in advanced jinking and jiving had taken them a good distance from the road and the bunkers they'd been aiming to inspect when the SAMs interrupted. Mongoose kicked the throttle open and slipped the A-10A into a straight tack north, calculating a new plan of attack as he went. The brown ribbon that marked the highway gradually grew wider. He decided they would cross it, then slide down out of the northwest.

Shotgun caught him as they reached the road. They angled northwestward, making just over 380 knots.

Combat did weird things to time. The actual encounter with the surface-to-air missiles hadn't lasted more than two or three minutes, yet it seemed to fill several hours. Everything immediately before it felt like it had happened days ago. Everything now felt like slow motion.

And yet, sitting on the strip at King Khalid, waiting for clearance—that seemed to have just happened. Mongoose glanced at his pocket where the letter was, then reached his hand over and patted it, as if for luck.

He'd left his wife feeding their baby in the living room. He'd kissed her, kissed him, kissed her again. He walked backwards to the door. A leather and fabric duffel bag sat there, worn from a thousand hellos and good-byes. Through the screen door he could see his ride waiting impatiently by the curb.

He lingered, watching her feed their baby, Robby. The infant's eyes were closed. The deep frown of worry on his wife's face gradually faded as she stared at her child.

"Hey, are those your bunkers at two o'clock?" asked Shotgun. "Shit, look at that. Goddamn Saddam's got a used-car lot down there. And I'm in the market for a flamed-out APC."

Mongoose's head nearly hit the canopy as he snapped back to the present. He tacked south a second, aiming to come back and orbit the site from above. Shotgun, following off his right wing in a loose trail, actually had a better position behind him as they turned. "You see any Scuds in there?" the major asked.

"Negative. I think the report was wrong."

"Maybe."

"Screw the Scuds," said Shotgun. "I say we dust these motherfuckers. We're gonna run out of sun in less than a half hour."

"Yeah, hang loose," Mongoose told him. "Let me think this one through a second."

They had given the area a fairly thorough search without finding the Scud site. Sunset was rapidly approaching. Tough hombre or no, the Hog was not a night fighter. He relayed the information back to the ABCCC controller, telling him that they had come up blank on the Scuds but found something almost as juicy. Unless someone aboard the C-130 had serious objections or a better read on the Scuds, they were going to expend their stores against the parking lot and then go home.

The controller was juggling about ten million things at once. By the time he cleared Devil flight to make the attack, Mongoose had blueprinted the raid three times. He noted what were probably two four-barrel antiair guns at each end; neither had activated its radar, either out of smart tactics or, more likely, because the Hogs were well out of range and hadn't been spotted. Assuming they were ZSU-23's—the most common antiaircraft guns the Iraqis had—the weapons would have to be respected, but were not an insurmountable problem, especially at medium altitude.

What he'd seen as a bunker was actually a low-slung building; it could be the top of an underground complex, though of course there was no way of really knowing from here. He debated using the Mavericks against it on the chance that it would hold ammunition and make a really spectacular boom. But the building wasn't going anywhere; it could be attacked whenever the targeters back at Black Hole wanted to hit it. The trucks and tanks—two or three seemed to be dug into shallow trenches—were a different story.

Mongoose would descend to ten thousand feet and use the Mavericks on the tanks. If the flak guns got annoying, they could go after them with the cluster bombs; otherwise, the GBUs would be dropped on the trucks. They'd hold off using the Hogs' cannons—and dropping below eight thousand feet—unless absolutely necessary, as per the general rules of engagement.

"I'm going to roll and take the vehicles furthest from the building," he told Shotgun. "I think they're tanks. Come around and see what's left."

"Copy."

"Watch your altitude and don't get too low. Keep your eye on that dune where the ground turns into the real desert. You see it?"

"I'm with you."

"Got to be a ZSU. You see that one and the other one?"

"Yeah. I'll let you know if they open up shop."

Mongoose came around in a half circle, lined up before he pushed over into a rolling dive, swinging the nose of the plane toward his target. He could see the three tanks clearly now, their guns pointing east rather than south.

The sand heaped around them would provide some protection against a near miss. But he wasn't going to miss. He felt his way into a thirty-five-degree glide, the turret of the tank at the right end inching toward the center of his screen. Mongoose moved his eyes to the Maverick's small targeting screen, probing for the heart of the shadow in the middle of the screen, sucked there like the tip of a compass seeking north. The cursor wobbled, then stuck, glued itself right in the center of the turret.

Mongoose held his stick dead steady and pickled, felt the Maverick slip away, and blinked his eyes, pulling the next missile on-line. He had to work the crosshairs hard, nearly lost his target, and realized his altitude was burning off faster than he'd planned; he was nearing eight thousand and was going to fall lower before he could fire. His recovery would probably bring him within range of well-managed AAA, but it couldn't be helped; he was going to have that tank. Finally the cursor slipped in and he had a lock and the missile was off, winging toward the lollipop that marked the top of the northernmost vehicle.

He moved his eyes up to the canopy, scanning the ground as he leveled off and began orbiting to the south. He missed seeing the first missile hit but caught the second: a small, almost insignificant splotch of brown and black flared into the shape of a procino mushroom and then quickly flattened, as the top of the tank jerked up and down as if it were a warm can of soda being opened.

The sky below his left wing began filling with black puffs of flak. In the same instant he realized the desert undulations had hidden two gun positions almost directly beneath his egress path.

12

Shotgun called the flak location about two seconds after it began, warning his lead to take evasive action. In the same moment he adjusted his course to eliminate the threat. He was at ten thousand feet with a clear view of the muzzle flash—it was a four-barrel ZSU-23, firing far too short to do any damage. Still, it had fired on a Hog, and its fate was sealed. He switched the Maverick's TVM to six-times magnification; his target was dead center. He locked and fired, then looked up in time to see the two other emplacements begin firing as well.

He wasn't in the best position to take out either one, so he put them on hold, deciding to use his last AGM-65B on the remaining tank instead. It was already lined up in the TVM, just about blinking "kill me." Nudging the cursor onto the big sucker, he locked and fired, the missile clunking off his wing with a sharp note of enthusiasm—one thing you could say about Mavericks, they sure liked to blow shit up.

Shotgun hit his armament panel to ready the cluster bombs as he recovered from the shallow dive. His altimeter read seven thousand feet, still well above the flak, though too low to drop the preset Rockeyes.

"Saddam's going to have a fire sale tomorrow," he told Mongoose, whose tail appeared on his left as he climbed to get into a better position. "I count three dead tanks and one busted flak-feeder."

A dusty haze covered the ground, making it difficult to see what was left. Two big bubbles of black flak boiled well off his right wing as the Iraqi gunners did their best to shoot themselves out of ammunition. The Hogs wheeled above the site, moving into a circle approximately 180 degrees from each other.

The ZSUs were starting to annoy him, and made it tough to target the rest of the site besides. Shotgun realized he was better oriented than Mongoose to splash them, and told his lead he would take them out.

"I can get them both on one swing. Then we can shoot up what's left downstairs."

"Go for it."

Shotgun pushed the Hog into a dive, tightening his attack angle into a steep plunge, the A-10 screaming down at close to ninety degrees. He was going to pee on these bastards. No one shot at a Hog and got away with it.

Bastards started dishing serious flak in his direction. The Hog snorted. She knew she was being fired at, and it pissed her off. She held her wings and tail stiff, urging her pilot to drop the Rockeyes and giving him an iron-stiff platform to do it from.

Shotgun pickled two of his four bombs on the first battery. Immediately he realized he hadn't adjusted properly for the wind. But it was too late; cursing, he pulled the stick back, determined to reset himself quickly for another attack. The Hog angrily slid her tail around, spanking the pilot for his miscue. But the CBUs were very forgiving weapons. A total of 187 spiked grenades, originally designed as armor-piercing weapons, peppered out from each bomb. Though the majority were well wide, enough fell close enough to silence the gun.

"There's another gun or something under netting on the northeast corner," said Mongoose as Shotgun got ready to pounce on the remaining gun. "Shit—you see that?"

Shotgun twisted his neck like a pretzel, trying to see what

Mongoose was talking about. By the time he figured it out, his commander had his nose just about on it. The Iraqis had done an excellent job of camouflaging the site defenses; there seemed to be another pair of ZSU-23's, or maybe larger-caliber guns, covered by the latest in desert wear.

"Hell of a lot of defenses for some old trucks," said Shotgun. "You think Saddam's got one of his whores in that bunker or what?"

"Could be."

"Probably screwing her right now."

"I'm on that gun."

He watched Mongoose dive into the attack just as the Iraqi gunner opened up. This was a big gun, probably a ZSU-57; the black wall of its shells appeared nearly twice as high as the others, though they were a bit behind Devil One's flight path. Suddenly the nose of the Hog veered upwards and to the left; two thin cigars plummeted past the swinging stream of antiaircraft fire toward the position. The canisters burst with a spectacular pop, an entire Iowa cornfield doing the Jiffy Pop thing as the double-barreled gun and its crew got perforated.

Mongoose wasn't done—rather than breaking off the attack, he took his Hog just about sideways, lining up his last two CBUs on the last ZSU on the northwestern dune. A stream of red-hot metal engulfed the four-barreled cheese grater and the black cloud of flak it had been dishing suddenly disappeared.

"Double bang," Shotgun told his lead before pushing into his own attack against the trucks.

This time, the Hog just about did the wind calculation for him, nudging its tail up and screaming when it was time to fire. A row of transports turned into molten dust.

"How's your fuel?" Mongoose asked as Shotgun fell into an easy orbit above the smoking debris.

Shotgun glanced at the dash. "Twenty minutes linger time, give or take a century," he said.

"Few more vehicles down there. You feel like cranking up your cannon?"

"Does a private shit in the woods?"

But as he slid around to get ready to cover Mongoose,

something caught his eye. He let the Hog drift a bit as his gaze found a hard-packed road. Five, six miles off, it headed toward a highway.

Something was happening there, something just beyond his vision.

Shotgun felt a twinge in his nose, as if he'd just caught a whiff of late-season Brazilian coffee beans being fresh roasted.

"Hey, Goose, hang tight a minute while I check something out," he radioed, pushing the Hog to follow the road. The terrain below gradually became less of a desert and more a generic waste, though it didn't look like anybody would be farming there soon.

The road led back north to the highway, where it plunged below it. A line of trucks was just now pulling off the paved road, kicking off a bunch of dust as they moved.

"Say, Goose, we got some sort of action going on south there, say three o'clock. You see that road?"

Mongoose broke his orbit and slid south, trailing Shotgun. They were still a good way off as the last truck in the caravan dipped off the highway, disappearing beneath the underpass.

It was a trailer type of truck, with a long, roundish cylinder in the back.

The sort of cylinder you made a missile out of.

No wonder they hadn't found the Scuds. The Iraqis had moved them.

13

Mongoose yanked at the stick angrily, mad that they'd wasted so much time and ammunition on the desert parking lot. Both planes had only their cannons left—excellent weapons, but it was going to be harder than hell to get a good shot at the bastards under the overpass.

Not really. Not at all. Hell, they'd done this sort of thing maybe a hundred times in training, working over highways throughout Europe. Not one underpass ever got away. All he had to do was take the Hog down to where it was designed to operate, and the missiles would be easy pickings.

Granted, they weren't supposed to fly so low. But Scuds overrode everything.

Besides, he wasn't flying a stinking Strike Eagle or a B-52. He was in a Hog.

Mongoose mapped a quick plan—low-altitude scream and pop, quick away, then up for the border, head for a tanker track directly south instead of KKMC. The tanker contingency was a nod to their dwindling fuel supply and any problems that might follow their close encounter of the Scud kind.

Shotgun practically took his ear off with a war whoop

when he told him they were going to nail the bastards at fifty feet.

"See, this is what I'm talking about," said his wingman. "This is the way to fight with a Hog."

Mongoose could feel the mask pinching his jaw as he worked to keep his voice flat. "We'll swing back and use what's left of the sun," he told his wingmate. "It's lined up almost perfectly. Let the fucking chips fall where they may."

"Yeah, I'm on you. Show me the way."

The flight leader marked the INS and gave the ABCCC the location. Then he swung northwest, working to get into position to make a straight-on shot up the road, sun at his tail. He began picking up momentum, energy and speed fanning each other as the plane revved herself toward a feeding frenzy.

"Ready?" he asked Shotgun as he geared into the attack.

"I was born ready."

Mongoose felt the plane roar as her nose sniffed out the underpass. The ground became a pebbly blur, the asphalt of the highway a thick black arrow pointing her toward hell. Mongoose sorted out the target area ahead in his wind-screen, working his eyes deliberately, slowing the world down so he could nail the crap out of it. The underpass was very wide and deep, maybe even designed from scratch as a bunker area. There were three support vehicles in the front on his right, lighter trucks that as far as he was concerned were mere annoyances. Two Scud carriers were at the left end of the thick underpass. There was a big cloud of dust and sand beyond the roadway, a tractor or something moving. The terrain rose to the right; he saw more activity there, a truck moving around.

If there was going to be any air defense, it would be there. His RWR was clear, but shit, at this altitude, a guy with a water pistol could get a bead on you.

The pilot blew a long, hard wad of air from his mouth, trying to control his adrenaline. Anger rumbled through his stomach—he wanted to nail the Scuds and wring Saddam's neck personally.

Bad.

Push the buttons and do your job. Checklist mode. Getting angry got you killed.

He was at two hundred feet, nearly dead on. He kept coming, nose in the dirt, eyes starting to itch, a vague pinch around the edges of his body, partly from the increasing g's and partly from tension. He edged right slightly, felt himself falling into that perfect space, his spine aligned with the plane's spine. The missile carriers had grown from distant cigarettes to thick, enticing sausages, to big fat targets filled with very combustible fuel.

Mongoose squeezed the trigger, the gun growling an angry roar as its one-and-a-half-pound charges leapt toward the enemy. The pilot leaned into the trigger, his eyes following the smoke. He gave the ship rudder to hold the line of bullets into the rear of the missile truck nearest the road. The force of the gun was so awesome it held the Hog back, slowing it in midair so that the plane seemed to hang around him, defying all laws of gravity and motion.

The underpass evaporated beneath the onslaught. Mongoose pushed his aiming point to the right without a clear target, searching for the next missile. He fired and he fired, and finally the Scud's rear fin or something was there, right in the middle of his bullets. He fired some more and he thought he could feel the heat of his gun. The plane rocked with the cannon, everything jumbling into one tremendous quake. He'd nailed the rear units of both missiles.

Webbed in the fine fuzz of total concentration, Mongoose pushed himself and the plane to get away. His throttle was full out as he zoomed away, beyond the attack.

It was a vulnerable moment; he was moving quickly but well framed against the horizon. He pushed his stick and kicked his rudders and bent his body hard to the right, hitting flares as a precaution against a shoulder-fired weapon, bolting from the bubbling cauldron of fire and burning sand. They were shooting at him, all Iraq was trying to kill him; even if their bullets were puny, a bullet was a bullet. He held the throttle full bore, hell-bent on getting away, skimming the ground low enough to count grains of sand. Finally sensing he was clear, Mongoose started to nose up, grabbing for more sky. He felt his chest muscles relaxing. There was a vehicle now he hadn't seen here along the highway; they were firing too, a lot of shit reaching out for him, but nothing he couldn't handle. He pushed the plane to get around, to get back and cover Shotgun's run.

He'd smashed the crap out of Saddam, nailed both Scuds. Who knows but maybe the stinking chemical crap the bastard intended dumping on the Americans or maybe the Israelis was now wafting below, killing his own men.

Served them right.

Mongoose took a long, relaxed breath, the easiest since they had crossed the border, and keyed his mike to tell Shotgun he could start his pass.

In that second, something thumped behind him, and he felt a flutter in his stomach that extended all the way back to his engines.

14

Shotgun shouted when he saw the flash from the far end of
the underpass. By then it was far too late for anything he
could do to have much of an effect, but he didn't think about
that. He keyed his mike to give the warning, and in
practically the same motion pushed the nose of his plane
down and smashed the trigger, hoping that his flailing
bullets would suppress any more fire. He couldn't hold the
angle well enough to nail the target, which passed by in a
blur; he tried rolling and diving back, but even Shotgun
could only bend Newton's laws so far. He got a good
glimpse of the bastard, though—a Roland SAM launcher,
sitting atop an AMX tank chassis and just about ready to
dish up another missile.

At him.

He yanked the Hog hard to the north, goosing the throttle
and hunkering down, wondering why the Scuds hadn't
caused a big enough explosion to take out the Rolands. The
Hog's ECM unit was useless against the missile's Siemens
J-band low-PRF tracking radar, which used techniques
perfected well after the pod came on line. All he could do
was jink and fly like hell.

Shotgun keyed his mike and shouted his warning to Mongoose again, then concentrated on his own plane, his own body, pushing it away. He had the throttle to the firewall; the Hog leapt forward with the lust of a race horse leaving the gate. He let the plane have her head for a few seconds, then took another hard turn, rolling out at the same time and just about cracking the plane's back as he whacked it sideways, exploring new dimensions in geometry. He flew the Warthog harder than an aerobatics plane, pushing it over and under and back again, trying to undo the knot the SAM had tied.

The Roland could move just over Mach 1.6. She had a limited range, though; he could win if he could run just a little further.

He glanced back and saw it coming for him, just about softball size and getting bigger in the rear quarter of his canopy.

Maybe he didn't see it at all; maybe this imagination was painting it there for him, because no way in real life you could see a Roland this long after it had been fired. He'd gone what? Ten miles at least. And still he felt the damn thing homing in on his head like Saddam had painted a big bull's eye there.

No way it could still be coming for him. Damn thing weighed less than 150 pounds, and it couldn't all be fuel.

He jinked again, this time so low to the desert floor he would have had to look up to change the oil on a Jeep. There was a thud or something behind him; the Hog seemed to gain speed. Shotgun pushed his stick hard and held on, fingers crossed, one more gut-smearing turn before he was finally sure that the cloud of dirt and shrapnel represented the last remains of the French and German missile.

Shotgun blew a breath and caught a glimpse of Mongoose's plane, well east and much higher than his, flying in the opposite direction toward Kuwait.

"Jesus, Goose, I thought they got you," he told his wingmate.

Devil One continued to climb to the east, rising from its run as easily as if it were on a training mission. The ugly dark green shades of camo smudged into a black blur, its pug nose and fat tail as pretty as a black Ferrari steaming around a racetrack. The late sun gleamed off the front of the canopy, its glint refracted into reddish-white fingers of light.

Then he saw the Hog waddle in the air, its left wing flailing upwards, out of the pilot's control.

Most of the other wing was gone. One or both of the missiles had blown right through it.

"Bail out, Goose!" Shotgun called. "Bail the fuck out!"

15

The emergency indicator lights were on, the engine was screaming, the plane was trying to pull herself over.

Hit.

Engine, must be. Right side.

Checklist mode.

Compensate for the dead engine, push the rudder, hold the stick.

Wing took something too.

Rudder not responding. Hydraulics out. Go to manual reversion.

Shit, there's no plane here.

Manual reversion.

Is there time?

Checklist mode.

Caution panel dotted with more lights than a power-grid station.

Controls still not doing their job.

Blue sky ahead.

Airspeed dropping.

Still climbing.

Momentum's a beautiful thing. Still moving somehow.

Stick feels like it's not connected.

Do I have Kathy's letter?

Restart the other engine.

Not this slow, no way.

Five thousand goddamn feet, a miracle to be this high.

Pointing north. Wrong direction.

Shit, no wing.

Can't hold it.

Have to jump now while the jumping is good.

Shame to leave this old Hog. Hell of a plane. Rescued from the scrap heap to whup Saddam's butt.

Got two Scuds at least.

Less than three seconds passed from the moment he was hit until Mongoose's eyes shot down toward the big yellow ejector loops at the edge of the ACES II seat. His body was still going through the motions, but his head was already outside the plane.

Eject. Eject.

He reached up and made sure his crash visor was down, hard hat secure, passport punched.

Eject. Eject.

He felt a soft pop, then closed his eyes as a powerful force yanked his legs back and pushed him against the seat. Wires below were severed by razor knives as the canopy blew out with a rush and the space below him exploded with a mad froth. Mongoose felt himself hurled upwards, enveloped in an icy whirlwind, then wrapped in a dark, blank void beyond time or place.

16

Shotgun pulled eight or nine g's in the turn, whacking the Hog down into the dust and going like all hell. He had to take out that Roland or no way anybody could get close enough to pick up Mongoose when his chute landed.

He saw, or thought he saw, an ejection, even though Mongoose didn't acknowledge. He'd have to go back for him; the Roland had to be taken out first.

A nice little Spark Vark jamming plane flying overhead right about now would have been immensely convenient. That or an up-to-date ECM pod on the right wing where the ancient ALQ-119 was hanging.

But hell, Shotgun told himself. He didn't need that fancy stuff. He was flying a *Hog*.

He came at the site about twenty feet off the ground, so low and close he could see the Roland crew members working frantically on the top of the mobile missile launcher. They had rolled it out from under its hiding place, whether to reload or get away from the fire on the other end, he couldn't be sure.

And he really didn't care. Shotgun pressed his trigger and tore the hell out of the lightly armored piece of French dog meat framed by the roadway behind it. A dozen armor-piercing and high-explosive shells ripped through the tank chassis, the metal steaming with death. The four or five men who'd been atop it literally vaporized as the pilot sat on his trigger.

Some enterprising troops had set up a heavy machine gun at the edge of the packed dirt road about twenty yards beyond the overpass. Shotgun gave them the finger as he zoomed out, whipping back for a run at the Scud carriers. As he came back and started to get into position to take his aim, he saw that both missiles were lying in splinters beneath the underpass.

They'd been decoys.

No matter—he danced his bullets into the underpass as he galloped forward, working his pedals to rake the area right to left. Then he turned his attention to the machine gun, awarding his own personal medals of heroism to the soldiers manning it.

When he came around for another pass, all he saw were dead bodies.

One more quick turn revealed nothing else was moving. He started climbing, heading in the direction he had last seen Mongoose's plane take. As the Hog gained altitude, he turned his radio to the emergency band, hoping for a locator beacon.

All he heard was static.

17

He was in the hospital. His wife Kathy was lying in the bed, scrunched up, her face red.

She was grunting. The doctor was standing at the edge of the bed.

Robby was being born. He felt himself trembling, worried that something was going wrong. But the nurse who had been with them was smiling. He trusted her, more than the doctor.

"You have to push harder," the nurse told Kathy. "Get into this one."

Kathy looked at him. She didn't say anything, but he felt fear in her eyes.

"You can do it," he told her. He stepped forward and gripped her hand, pushing confidence into his voice. The wave hit her and she pressed against him, her muscles contracting to push their baby down the birth canal.

"Here," said the doctor. "You can feel his hair."

Major Johnson smiled as he let the doctor guide his fingers. The sensation was wet, oily even.

"That's your son."

The idea barely registered. The head slipped back inside Kathy's body.

"Here comes another one," said the nurse.

He leaned toward his wife, who raised her body with the push. She groaned and screamed and suddenly the baby squirted out, born, alive, his body all red. He looked like a wrinkled Martian.

Jesus, that's my son, Mongoose thought.

The vision snapped black. He whirled around, the moving eye of a tornado.

He was tumbling.

His visor and oxygen mask were in place, shielding his face somewhat, but still the wind was a sharpened icicle, chiseling at his head.

It was so cold that his nerve inputs couldn't process it all and told his brain that he was on fire. He was hot and frozen cold at the same time.

Mongoose thought about his arms and legs. It was easy to break them getting out of the plane. He tried to move them closer to his body, belatedly trying to protect them. The base of his skull hurt and his neck and shoulders burned.

A stiff, hard hand whacked him backwards. The breath ran out of him; by the time he could breathe again he saw that the ejection seat's drogue parachute had deployed. He was falling, but much slower now.

The wind was still a bitch. It was whipping cold against him, and dragging him east. But he was lucky—the seat's canister of emergency oxygen was making it easier to breathe, easier for him to clear his head.

The main chute kicked in. He fluttered, head whirling; he reached his hands to his chest and blanked again, momentarily.

Now surplus material, the seat that had saved him fell away. He had a vague notion that he was still moving forward in the air—he'd come out at an angle, propelled like a performer from a circus cannon, right over the big tent, way out past the parking lot. The sun shimmered in the hazy edge of the dirt a few yards away, as if it had gone out three seconds ahead of him and its chute had failed to open.

Mongoose felt the harness pulling against his body, his parachute being pulled up by a stiff wind. He felt like he was going faster than the damn airplane.

There was a way to steer. He knew how to steer, he'd practiced it before.

It hadn't been like this. The wind had been calmer and the air warmer, his heart beating much slower.

Checklist mode, he told himself. One item at a time.

"There's nothing in Iraq worth dying for."

Who had said that? General Horner? Colonel Knowlington?

Checklist mode. Item one—steer the chute away from the enemy. Steer south.

Assuming the sun still set in the west, he was already headed in that direction. The chute responded and moved even faster.

For a second he thought he might actually steer all the way back to Saudi Arabia.

But then the ground started moving faster than he did.

18

The thing was, there ought to be more smoke. A Hog going down ought to make a hell of a big splash. Tear a hole in the desert and send a half-million Iraqis to hell with it.

Here there was nothing, not even dust. Maybe a vague whisper of gray in the air around it, haze only.

Or a soul, taking one last look at the bent body.

It was the Hog, though, no question. Even with the light fading, Shotgun could see the wing section flat against the sand. The end had sheered and mangled, but a good hunk of it was intact.

Hell, you could probably dust it off, bang out the dents, and put it on another plane, no sweat.

Couldn't do that with the fuselage. It lay in a twisted tumble almost a mile away, crunched worse than a candy-bar wrapper. The plane had been a trooper to the end, flying nearly ten miles before finally pancaking.

No way Mongoose would have survived that.

He'd gone out, though. Shotgun knew he had. He had a memory of seeing a seat vaulting in the air.

Or at least, he saw how it should have happened. And at the moment, that was good enough for him. Because any other way, his lead was snuffed. They were damn close to the Euphrates, way far north in bad-guy territory at the edge of the desert, within gum-spitting distance to the Republican Guard. No way Mongoose was catching it here, no way. Guy was going to live to a ripe old age and bounce grandkids off his knee.

So where was he now? The survival radio didn't seem to be broadcasting. Shotgun keyed his own mike a few times, hoping for an answer.

Worst case, the radio ought to at least be putting out a locator beacon. Mongoose carried two, so he had a backup.

Nada.

Shotgun rode his Hog higher in the sky, scanning the ground for a parachute. By now the sun had set and the desert was starting to turn into a twilight fog. Wind whipped the spots of loose dirt below, making it even harder for him to see.

But hell, anybody could spot a stinking parachute.

Shotgun saw a clump of trees and scrub vegetation to his northwest, and another to his east. He rocked over both in a wide figure-eight, but found no one.

A trio of squat buildings sat about two miles south of the wrecked plane. He investigated them next, flying low enough to read the number on the mailboxes.

If there had been mailboxes. All three buildings were in shambles, roofs blown off. There was a narrow road nearby, not so much a road as a path, dirt of a different color.

Shotgun checked his radio and keyed the mike again.

"Yo, Goose. How's it hanging?"

Still nothing.

Maybe he hadn't seen him eject.

Damn it, Mongoose was alive. Stink-ass Iraqis could not *kill* a Hog driver. No, sir. Hog driver was a serious entity, not quite superhuman, but not susceptible to fingernail-breaking crap like this.

Even if the missile had been a NATO job. Better than the Russian crap, but still not good enough to take out a Hog driver, especially Mongoose. He was an anal son of a bitch who played engineer in the cockpit, painting by numbers and more careful than a goddamn Girl Scout.

Well, almost. Point of the matter was, he was a kick-ass pilot and squadron DO besides, and could *not* be taken off the board by the Iraqis.

Most likely, he was hiking back to the Saudi border by now. Probably halfway home. Maybe even sitting at the bar in the Depot, ordering a double bourbon.

On the rocks.

Shotgun edged the Hog higher, pointing the nose southeast, as if he really did expect to find the flight leader hiking in the sand below. There was a town, or at least a group of buildings that could be a town, six or seven miles further east, back in the direction of Kuwait. Mongoose would stay away from that, for sure, but would the people there stay away from him?

"Devil Two, this is Red Dog. We have two Vipers approaching your location. Stand by for frequency."

Shotgun waited impatiently for the airborne controller to read off the numbers. He would have preferred a pair of Hogs instead of the F-16 "Vipers" or "Falcons," but the fast movers would have to do; he was running low on fuel and would have to leave soon to tank.

The single-engined fighters were using the call sign "Boa," as in boa constrictor. Shotgun snorted when he made contact, but didn't bother commenting on the cuteness of the name. You had to expect that sort of thing in a pointy-nose.

The irony of snakes hunting up a Mongoose, well, that was a different story. That was almost karma.

"Boa One to Devil Two, do you have a location on the emergency beacon?"

"Negative. I have the plane, but I haven't made contact." He ignored their ominous silence, reading off an INS marker and giving them a vector as he picked up their location.

"You sure he got out?" asked Boa One as the two fly-by-wire jockeys approached.

"Bet your fucking ass he did."

"Hey, relax, buddy. We're on your side, remember? We'll find him."

Shotgun didn't answer.

The two F-16's, diverted from another mission, were

flying at about eighteen thousand feet. Using the buildings and the wrecked Hog as landmarks, he sketched the area out for them. Even though they were pointy-nose types, they seemed relatively good-natured. They had no problem putting their chins down to get a good look at things.

Eagle pilots, though, those guys would cop attitude. Now that would be something to deal with.

He checked his fuel. Even an optimistic run at the math left him with two minutes less flying time than it would take to find a tanker.

But hell, this was a critical moment. Night was coming on, and no way Goose had thought to pack his flannels. Somebody had to find him and fast.

But really, if Shotgun waited much longer before going for gas, he was going to join him on the ground. That wasn't much help.

It wasn't like he was leaving Mongoose alone up here. The ABCCC had tasked a force to sponge the area clean of any more Iraqi missiles hiding in the bushes; the sky was starting to get busy. Shotgun knew that Special Ops troops working with Air Force Pave Lows had been tasked to air-rescue operations. Shotgun had a high opinion of the Green Berets—and their coffee, which he had helped himself to during a visit to one of their forward air bases a few days ago.

But even *they* couldn't mount a rescue if the pilot was nowhere to be found. The crews had orders not to cross into Iraq until the man was found and verified.

One more pass, then he'd tank. He made sure the volume on the radio was full blast as he edged the Hog down, running along the dark ribbon of a road not far from the buildings.

Why the hell didn't Mongoose use his radio?

"Yo, Goose, come on, buddy, this is Gun. I promise I'll share my Big Mac pack with you tonight."

Boa One asked if he had something. Shotgun let the static fuzz in his helmet before telling the Viper pilot that he thought he'd seen a glint on the ground.

"Roger that. We'll take a pass. Controller's trying to get

you," relayed the pilot. "They're thinking you should be returning to base before you run your tanks dry."

"Well, screw them."

"Yo, man, I'm just the messenger," answered the pilot. "But running out of fuel isn't going to help your buddy."

Shotgun punched the Hog down for a last peek at the abandoned buildings, hoping he might find Mongoose doing jumping jacks on what was left of the roof. Beyond the building, he gave the control yoke an angry yank to put his nose skyward. The Hog groaned a bit, complaining that it wasn't its fault Mongoose had gone down.

He spotted another pair of F-16's circling just to the west. They had been sent to make sure the Scuds were toast, and to mop up any remaining SAMs.

"Okay, guys, I'm going to go tank," Shotgun told Boa One. "I'll be back ASAP."

"Don't sweat it," said the pilot. "Your guy'll be back at base draining beers in no time. And for the record, I prefer a quarter-pounder with cheese."

"Copy that," Shotgun told him, plotting his course to the nearest tanker.

19

When he landed, Mongoose felt his knee give slightly. But he was already well into the roll, already peeling over. He tumbled onto his side, thought for a second that he was going to roll forever, realized the chute's harness was still attached, and wondered why he hadn't released it. He had dirt in his mouth. He pushed himself forward, put weight on the knee, and again thought of the chute. One hand began reaching for his knife as the other slipped the harness restraints.

Okay, he told himself, calm down. The hard part is over; all you have to do is wait for the search-and-rescue helicopter. Just relax. Push your buttons.

Remove the radio from your vest. Turn it on. Very simple. Very calm.

Breathe first.

No one answered his first hail.

He was having trouble talking anyway, still gulping air. He put his hands to his chest and steadied a slow breath in and out. Making sure his finger was on the microphone button, he tried again.

He gave his call sign, asked for a response. Something floated in, a mangled transmission from far off; there was too much static for him to make any sense of it.

Bits and pieces of his SERE—Survival, Evasion, Resistance, and Escape—training came back to him as his mind slowly cleared. The first few minutes on the ground were critical. You wanted to keep yourself in control.

Push your buttons. Check your list.

He was going to be picked up. It was just a matter of keeping his head clear.

Damned if there hadn't been a shitload of rain during his SERE training. And heat. Now it was just cold.

And in a desert, or actually on the edge of one. You'd think it would just be hot all the time.

Mongoose tried the radio again. Its range varied according to weather, terrain, and time of day, but he could probably count on about thirty miles. Planes could zip in and out of its envelope without getting a good fix; he tried to keep it straight up and down for maximum range, speak slowly as he transmitted, stay calm.

His head was still foggy. He had only a vague notion of where he'd been hit, relative to his target. It was well south and east, he knew that. And after he had gone out he'd flown through the sky like a missile, away from the plane.

His breathing was starting to come back under control. He thumbed his radio to a new frequency, took it from the top.

From the air, much of southern Iraq looked almost featureless, undulating sand and gristly dirt extending for miles and miles. Here on the ground, Iraq turned out to be a silty waste, tiny grains of sand and grit sifting among stubby branches, as if the desert had flooded an orchard. A rough progression of hills began immediately to his right, long bumps nudging back north; they could have been part of an ancient stairway leading to the Euphrates, worn down by time. A dry creek bed or wadi lay about a hundred feet ahead of him, its gully oriented approximately east-west. A hard-packed road skirted close to it about twenty yards from where he was standing. Beyond the road, the terrain seemed a little harder. There were several clumps of short trees and more hills.

Wind kicked up grit and slapped his cheeks as he tried the radio again, reminding him that every transmission by the PRC-90 emergency radio in theory helped the enemy as much as would-be rescuers. He had to ration his calls, at least until he was sure someone was coming for him.

He'd have to ration his water too. He had only his pocket canteen and four packets in his vest.

Mongoose took out the small canteen and sipped very slowly. But the sips were larger than he thought; it took only three to drain the container.

Shotgun ought to be around up there somewhere. No way Shotgun would have left him. He repeated his hail and then switched to beacon, setting the radio to emit a distinctive SOS that in theory all allied planes could recognize.

Any Iraqi who wasn't blind had probably seen him land. He had to get the hell out of here.

He'd thrown his helmet off after he'd gotten to his feet. It lay upside down a short distance away, looking a bit forlorn. His chute had tangled in the stubby vegetation. The ejection seat, its emergency survival pack, and life raft were all set out like props upstage in a surreal play.

He ought to hide what he didn't need, even if it was getting dark. Anything left in the open would point the Iraqis toward him, when they came.

As he stared at the seat, he felt a pain in the back of his head. It was like a fist pounding from the inside, whacking at the base of his skull and neck. He put his fingers into the wedge behind his ears, tried to relieve the pressure by kneading the muscles there. Closing his eyes, Mongoose attempted once again to control his breathing, slowing it and relaxing all his muscles, hoping to ease whatever spring had overwound itself. His body was starting to shake, whether from shock or the cold he couldn't tell. He wanted to take stock of his survival supplies and equipment, but all he could think of for nearly a full minute was the pain. A shock-induced trance was slowly taking hold of him.

The sound of an approaching truck on the roadway knocked him out of it.

20

Colonel Knowlington was still going over the A-10A check flight when Captain Bristol Wong's perpetual frown appeared over Sergeant Rosen's shoulder. Wong was a rarity—an intelligence officer who was actually intelligent and had a sense of humor. His dry, anti-bureaucratic wit was so funny that just looking at his face generally made Knowlington start laughing.

Not today, though. Wong's face was drawn and worried, and Knowlington knew exactly what the problem was as soon as he approached.

"Colonel, you want to get on with Lieutenant Dixon at Riyadh right now, sir," Wong told him.

Knowlington nodded, and without saying or doing anything else, immediately began walking toward his office in the squadron building. An A-10A fresh from combat screeched onto the runway, but he didn't hear it. Nor did he see any of the several people who greeted him as he walked. He walked in a gray, cold space alone, nerve endings hardened, ready though not enthusiastic about doing his duty.

He didn't even greet Dixon when he came on the line. All he said was, "Who is it?"

"Looks like Major Johnson in Devil One," said the lieutenant. "I'm still pulling in details. It was their last mission of the day. Their tasking was changed and they went after Scuds about sixty miles further north. I happened to be in—"

"He eject?"

"I don't know, sir."

Knowlington nodded but said nothing, as if his lieutenant could see his response.

"What else do you know, BJ?"

"Nothing, really," said the lieutenant, "Shotgun's still up there. They have a search-and-rescue operation going, but I don't have any details. I don't know that he's been heard from. In fact, I kind of think he wasn't. But I wasn't, well, obviously back here—"

"I understand, BJ. I appreciate your getting the word to me right away on this."

"I thought you guys might have heard something."

"Not yet. Most of the squadron's just coming in."

"You want me to . . ."

Dixon's voice trailed off, most likely because he didn't know exactly what to offer. Knowlington told him just to keep his ears open, but otherwise to go about his normal routine. The colonel had more than enough sources, formal and informal, to fill in all the blanks on his own.

"Thanks for calling me," the colonel told him. "Look, don't piss anybody off over there. I'm going to get you back ASAP."

"Yes, sir. Thank you."

Knowlington just barely resisted the impulse to shove the phone through the wall. Mongoose had been diverted sixty miles further north? Shit, why not just send him up to Baghdad and get it over with?

Sending Hogs that far into enemy territory was contrary to just about every lesson the Air Force had learned since Eddie Rickenbacker got his sights on a German biplane. The plane had been specifically built for close-in ground support. Because of that, she was slow, didn't carry much in the way of sophisticated ECMs, and was unsuited for anything but low-altitude tactics.

She was a fantastic tank-buster and a hell of a ground-attack meat-grinder; the Army loved her. The men who flew her rated as some of the best stick-and-rudder jocks Knowlington had ever met.

But. Send her on missions deep into Injun territory, and eventually you were bound to lose her. This wasn't a black jet or a Strike Eagle you were talking about here.

Knowlington had written something like that in a report many years back, when the Hog's viability was being studied and he was pulling an unwished-for stint on someone's evaluation staff.

He had, in fact, recommended the plane be phased out.

Ancient history.

But the missions on Day One of the air war had been just as deep, and he had gone along with them. Where was his head then?

More to the point, why did he let someone else lead them? Over-the-hill or not, it was his job, his duty, as commander to be at the head of the line, not back. Screw anyone who had a different opinion.

And screw his other problems. He was beyond them.

Today anyway.

In his experience, the odds on recovery were a real downward curve against time—the quicker you made radio contact, the better the odds of a good extraction. The problem was, things had a tendency to go less than perfectly. In the first rush of landing, your head got scrambled and even the most experienced pilot made poor decisions. Shock jumbled your brain in weird ways; he'd heard of guys who'd neglected to use their radios or flares, and even one who inflated his life raft and got aboard in the middle of a jungle.

It was getting late; if they hadn't already made contact with him, there was a real good chance Mongoose would be spending part of the night in Indian country.

Assuming he wasn't already a prisoner, or permanent resident.

Looking out his small office window at the steadily darkening sky, the colonel refused to consider those possibilities.

21

Mongoose dropped flat in the sand. He pushed up and saw the truck, still maybe a mile away on the road, then reached beneath him for his service pistol.

The 9mm Beretta was a serious gun, a good one, well cared for, meticulously cleaned at least once a day.

Hopefully he wouldn't have to use it. He tucked his elbows beneath his body and levered himself into a kneel and then a crouch. He looked toward the roadway and out into the wasteland. The blur driving toward him in the darkening twilight sharpened into a white pickup. It seemed out of place, and for a moment he felt a strange dislocation, as if instead of being in southern Iraq the wind had carried him all the way back to the States, over to Iowa or South Dakota.

Had the terrain looked a hair less desert-like, he might even have believed that.

Just because it was a pickup didn't mean that it wasn't an army truck. And even if it was being driven by a civilian, it still presented a very real danger. Most likely there was a price on his head.

Dead as well as alive.

The truck kept coming. The driver had his running lights on but not his headlights; probably he could see well enough without them since the sun had only just gone down. Besides, putting them on was an invitation to get smoked.

Mongoose felt his legs and back stiffening. The truck driver would have a clear view of him, assuming he looked in his direction.

He could easily be seen if he got up and ran. Best to stay still, hope the guy wasn't paying attention, or the shadows obscured him. Movement attracted the eye.

The Beretta had a faintly oily feel to it. It was warm in his hand, and heavy. He put his left hand around the right, giving himself a good, steady platform to fire from.

Mongoose had learned to shoot when he was ten, plinking cans with his dad's BB pistol in the backyard. He'd moved up to a .22 rifle, taken a gun safety and marksmanship course in the Boy Scouts. By the time he got to the service he'd become a reasonably accurate shot, even with a handgun. He might not be a marksman, but compared to most Air Force officers he was William Tell.

He had a good firing position, well anchored in the ground. If the guy stopped, he could smoke him. The road was less than ten yards away—a good shot with a pistol, but not spectacular.

Belatedly, the pilot thought of trying to hide. But there didn't seem to be any sense; it wasn't like he had enough time to dig a hole in the streambed.

It was his job to take out this guy.

No, his job was to survive. First rule, only rule.

Most likely, the guy would pass him by.

Farmer in Iowa, probably he'd be so focused on his work or where he was going or what was playing on the radio, he'd never notice someone crouching near the road.

But the truck started to slow.

Mongoose's mouth was dry. The gun was heavy in his hands; he tried to relax his arm muscles a bit, ignoring the pain in his head.

What could the guy have seen?

The plane? Sure, but that was miles away.

The chute?

Maybe. Falling objects did have a tendency to attract attention, even in Iraq.

The truck stopped directly in front of the wadi. It looked like a Toyota, five or six years old at least. Its front end was crimped and crinkled, and it had a dirty sheen to it.

It was ten yards away, even a little less.

The driver cranked down the window and looked at him. The man's face was illuminated by a dull glow from the instrument panel. It was unshaven, with a thick mustache but a spotty beard, black and grayish whiskers patched around his chin. He was wearing a white shirt and some sort of hat. He stared at Mongoose the way a man might stare at a tiger found in its cage on a city street.

I should smoke him, Mongoose thought.

Had the man gotten out of the truck, had he raised a gun to the window, the pilot would have brought his pistol up an inch and fired. There was no question of hitting him. Mongoose saw it all in a far corner of his mind, saw himself pumping the trigger four or five times, saw one of the slugs catching the man in the shoulder, wounding him only, but enough to stop him from getting away. Mongoose saw himself jumping up from the crouch, breath hot and shallow in his lungs, saw himself run and pump two bullets into the man's head.

He could have done all this, and he would have had the man done anything but stare. He would have done it without agonizing or even thinking much about it, because it was his job to survive. He would have done it because he had to.

But the man never moved toward him. He only stared from the truck, a voyeur in an unreal world. Mongoose stared back, equally out of place.

The hard thunder of an F-16 crossed into his consciousness. The plane was flying high, but very close.

The radio was on the ground. He'd have to take a hand off the gun to reach it.

Not possible.

Unless he shot the guy first. He should just squeeze the trigger and fire. Get him right through the open window, hit him in the face.

The man was looking at him with such a blank, open expression. Something like wonder, not hostility.

A real enemy. A real person.

They stared at each other as the fighter's noise faded. There was no question the Iraqi knew Mongoose didn't belong here, and no question that by now he would have realized there was a gun in his hands.

Any move, even opening the door, even waving hello, he'd smoke him.

But why didn't he just kill him now? He had a good, clean, clear shot.

Mongoose remained stock-still, his movements held in balance by a hair-thin thread of fate.

Finally, the truck started to ease forward. It moved slowly, only gradually picking up speed, continuing down the highway in the direction it had been going before stopping.

The pilot remained in his crouch until it had shrunk to the size of a worm in the distance. Slowly, carefully, he rose. He started to walk down the wadi, gingerly at first, then quickly, his legs falling into a trot.

For some reason he couldn't fathom, he stopped and looked both ways before crossing the empty highway.

22

Shotgun was next in line behind a Marine F/A-18. Thing was, the damn Marine wasn't used to sipping from an Air Force straw, and had trouble attaching to the hose at the tail end of the KC-135. It didn't take more than a minute, but Shotgun had never counted patience one of his virtues.

Still, he kept his curses to himself. Even if the guy was just a Marine, you didn't diss him in the air.

Certainly not when he was ahead of you in the tanking queue.

When it was his turn, Shotgun practically rammed his nose into the long nozzle at the back of the KC-135. The boomer, sitting in the rear of the plane and controlling the refueling apparatus, was supposed to do all the work, but Shotgun didn't have time to mess around; a case like this, he figured, they ought to have do-it-yourself service. Stick your credit card in the slot and pump it yourself.

The pilot thumped his leg with his hand as the fuel rushed into the Hog's empty tanks, trying to increase the flow with his own hurried beat. He was off the straw and cranking back toward Iraq faster than a kid skipping out on a bar bill.

Not that he didn't trust the F-16's to do a good job

looking for Mongoose and protecting him. It was just that some things were better done by a Hog.

The F-16C Fighting Falcon was a good aircraft, a fine all-around, all-purpose jet. Designed and first flown in the seventies, it had been built ground-up as a close-in dog-fighter, a lightweight plane that could actually out-duel an F-15 up tight and carry a full load of bombs through high-g maneuvers. Except for the odd position of the stick—it was alongside you instead of in front of you—it was a sweet thing to fly. There were a million of them in theater, doing everything from reconnaissance to combat air patrol to dumb bombing.

But they weren't Hogs. A Hog carried sixteen thousand pounds of bombs without thinking about it. A Hog lived in the mud. A Hog just flew and flew and flew.

And a Hog took care of its own. Part of the rescue package or not, equipped for night operations or not, Shotgun belonged there. Hell, he'd haul Mongoose into the helicopter himself if it came to that. Land in the desert, hop out, pitch him in, and take off again.

A-10 probably could do that. Just no one thought to try it yet.

Shotgun tracked back in a straight line, or as straight as any fighter pilot would fly riding into Injun territory without stealth or 120,000 feet between them and the ground.

"You're back?" Boa One asked as Shotgun returned to the area where Mongoose had gone down. "I thought you just left."

"Where's my guy?"

The Vipers hadn't heard a thing. They had scanned the wreckage pretty well, and gone low and slow—for F-16's—over the entire area. But they'd seen and heard nothing. Nor had any of the other assets.

Not good news.

Shotgun nosed the Hog down toward the mud, deciding to trace this thing out. First stop was the underpass where they had encountered the SAMs. The site had been re-pounded and it absolutely glowed, as if it were a radioactive dump.

As he approached, aiming to duplicate Mongoose's pass,

he saw a black shadow coming down the road. He nosed forward, made it as an Iraqi army vehicle, a deuce-and-a-half troop-type truck. He lit his cannon, splashing bullets into the thick Brillo pad of a vehicle. It veered off into the sand, and he caught the ground sparkle of the soldiers emptying their rifle clips at him as he started to pull off. The bullets helped him home in on the target despite the darkness; he pressed on and fired his own cannon, whacking the truck with a quick burst that ignited a pretty fireball from the gas tank.

The Viper pilots were jabbering in his ear as he pulled off, asking if he needed assistance.

"Next time," he told them, taking a quick orbit around the truck roast. When he was sure nothing was moving down there or nearby, he spun his plane in the direction he had last seen Mongoose taking. He couldn't be precisely sure of where the major had been, though, and the difference of a small angle would mean a lot.

Plus it was really dark now. Too dark to see with anything but his gut.

Here was the wrecked Hog, lying in pieces strewn across the earth.

Shotgun pushed his plane down, trying to get another look at the fuselage. He had to face the fact that Mongoose might not have gotten out.

He was going almost slow enough to land. Even so, there was no way to see anything more than a few mangled shadows. Three circuits and he still couldn't tell for sure if he'd really found the plane, let alone whether Goose was still in it.

For what felt like the millionth time, Shotgun keyed the emergency frequency, looking for his flight leader. The only answer was static.

He put the Hog at two thousand feet and made for the buildings again.

If Mongoose was down there, too much close attention like this would draw the enemy. But damn it, Shotgun had to find him so the helos could come and pick him up. All he needed was one little flare, and he'd have the choppers here in no time. They liked making their pickups in the dark.

The Boas handed off to a second pair of F-16's.

Still nothing.

"We're not giving up on you," the controller assured Shotgun when he suggested Devil Two return to base. "But, uh, you've been flying a long time now."

"I've got plenty of fuel."

"We copy, sir. We copy."

He didn't add "but," though it was clearly implied.

But.

But common sense said the longer Shotgun stayed up, the less efficient he was going to get. And hell, it was dark. The Hog was many things, but it wasn't a night fighter.

Shit, thought Shotgun, all I need is a damn flashlight.

At some point, even U.S. Air Force Captain Thomas O'Rourke had to be realistic. Common sense said that there was a reason they weren't getting a transmission from Mongoose.

Common sense said he wasn't going to find him in the dark. Sooner or later he would have to call it a day.

Shotgun keyed the emergency frequency again, then cut his throttle back ten percent, hoping to push later a bit further out.

23

Mongoose had walked nearly a half mile from the road, and begun to parallel it south toward a clump of low trees, before realizing that he had left the seat's survival pack back where he landed. He stopped, nearly slapping his forehead with his right hand, though he was still holding his pistol.

He spun around to go back, then stopped himself.

"Checklist mode," he said aloud. "Think, don't react."

To get the pack, he would have to cross the road again. It was getting truly dark and he might not make it back here, let alone to the trees. He wanted to be near them to direct the helo in when it came.

The seat pack had a spare radio, more flares. Mongoose debated whether they were worth getting. He already had a radio. He had his water, the gun, his knife, some flares. Going back would take at least a half hour, maybe more; he might or might not find his way.

If the Iraqis had found the chute and seat, they might be there now, setting an ambush or booby-trapping them.

He had to keep away from the enemy, make contact with an allied plane, and hang tight until the rescue team got there. The seat pack wasn't essential. It was a backup really. He could do without it.

Probably get picked up in a few minutes.

Mongoose felt a twinge in his knee as he squatted and holstered his gun. The pain at the back of his head had settled into a steady but low rhythm, vaguely reminiscent of the throb of an out-of-tune Chevy Camaro the pilot had owned as a teenager. He could live with the thump and his slightly strained knee; all things considered, he was in great shape.

The survival radio felt like a thin Walkman in his hand as he made another transmission. The squelch sounded a bit different, but there wasn't an acknowledgment. He flipped over to the beacon, broadcast a while, waited.

Shotgun would have the helos on their way. Best to find a landmark to steer them toward.

The trees. He started walking again.

When he was less than fifty yards from the shadows, they began to move. He stopped, drew his pistol, slid down into his crouch. Mongoose told himself it must be the wind, even though the movement seemed human. He rocked his upper body back and forth, scanning with the gun, waiting for the shadows to either stop moving completely or separate.

Neither happened. He straightened slowly, pulling the gun back close to his body. The trees were hardly tall enough to be worth calling them that; they had thin, bent trunks and scraggly tops. Not even a kid could have hidden behind them had there been daylight.

But in the dark their shadows were a thick blur. Though he'd been watching the copse for probably close to an hour now, Mongoose was no longer sure of it, or himself; he couldn't trust his eyes. He began sidestepping, moving to his right, gun still drawn against an ambush.

If an Iraqi soldier was hiding in the copse, he'd have wasted Mongoose by now. This distance with a rifle, he'd be diced.

Or maybe not. The guy might be scared, not know whether Mongoose was armed or not—might not even know he was the enemy.

Why would he be waiting then?

Mongoose ducked as he saw something move. He pushed the gun out, steadied it with both hands.

Nothing.

He sidestepped some more. The copse was small, with a half-dozen trees, its circumference twenty yards tops. The ground tilted toward it, as if it were a bottom of a bowl.

The night was as quiet as the inside of a funeral home at midnight.

Something moved again. This time Mongoose was sure it was a man taking aim at him, and fired.

The crack of the gun had a hollow sound that lasted for what seemed like hours, not an echo but the long strand of the only noise in a deep vacuum of silence. Mongoose strained to keep his finger from pushing the trigger again, waited for a muzzle flash to show him where to aim, felt sweat starting to drip across the back of his cheek, even though he was colder than he'd ever been in his life.

There was no muzzle flash. He resumed his sidestep, quicker now, knowing that if no one had returned his fire there was no one there, realizing the movement and shadows had only been his imagination, but still feeling his stomach boil.

When he had circled the copse, Mongoose pushed forward to the trees, closing his eyes as he passed between two trunks into the small clearing at its center. When no one rushed him, he opened them again and saw there was a small depression here, almost a trench. He plopped down and took one more look around, told himself aloud he was all right, then laid his pistol aside and yanked at his vest, grabbing for one of the water packets. He tore it clumsily and drank in a gulp, losing a good portion down his face and neck.

It took a lot to keep form ripping open another.

"You have to make this stuff last a while," he said to himself, again speaking out loud, though this time in a whisper. "It's your job."

Mongoose took his radio out and came up on the emergency frequency once again, broadcasting first in beacon mode and then voice.

Still no answer. He couldn't understand that. Except for the brief flutter when he first landed, the radio had been silent. There ought to be a good amount of traffic up here; certainly someone should be in range to pick him up.

Mongoose gave another burst, held the small radio to his ear, listening.

Was the damn thing even working? He could hear static. He shook it, listened again. Half the Air Force ought to be close enough to hear him.

Not to mention Shotgun.

Unless he'd been bagged too. Mongoose didn't know what had hit him; it had happened so fast he hadn't really been able to tell. He thought it was probably a shoulder-fired heat-seeker, even though there had seemed to be too much damage for that.

He stopped himself from replaying the hit. He had to stay in the present, the future. Mongoose tried the radio again, then checked his watch. He'd wait fifteen minutes before transmitting again. The battery wouldn't last forever.

It was possible that there was something wrong with it. He might be transmitting, but not receiving. Or some vagary with the altitude or clouds or sunspots or fate might be screwing him up.

Checklist mode.

He had to face the possibility that he was going to be spending the night.

A very strong possibility.

It was cold. The wind was starting up again, and that only made things worse.

This was the only sheltered area nearby, and any group of Iraqi soldiers would undoubtedly head for it if they were searching the area. He would have to leave it, go far enough away to be safe, but stay close enough to use it to guide the air-rescue chopper in if it came.

Not if. *When* it came.

Now the shadows of the trees felt comforting, as if they could protect him. And there was wood on the ground, maybe enough to start a small fire, something to keep warm.

Not enough wood to make it last very long. And it would definitely risk alerting the Iraqis.

The guy in the pickup might have taken care of that already.

The time to start the fire was an hour or two before dawn. He'd minimize his exposure to the Iraqis. Most of them would have given up searching by then, or at least taken a break.

But shit, he'd be frozen solid if he didn't do something to warm up.

The faint whisper of Hog fan-jets in the distance turned his head around with a jolt.

His imagination?

Or Shotgun, looking for him?

He listened again, trying to blank his mind. Nothing. It had been a trick of his imagination, a tease of fear, like the shadows.

Even so, he took out his flare set, loaded the small gun with a pencil flare, poised to fire.

Complete silence and not a moving shadow in the sky.

Checklist mode. Save the flare.

He hadn't eaten since breakfast, but he didn't feel hungry yet. Which was a fairly good thing—there were no Big Macs lying around, and the nearest falafel stand was quite a hike.

He had to leave the copse. He squatted down and began to re-inventory his gear, justifying the delay with the thought that it was the last time he might have a chance to do so before morning. He took each item out and placed it directly in front of him, the way a little kid might take stock of his Hot Wheels or baseball card collection. The ritual of touching each piece of equipment was comforting, reminding him that he had the tools to get out of this alive. Besides the survival radio and gun, Mongoose had a flashlight, three smoke-flares, the tiny flare gun and its bandolier of flares, a compass, a strobe light, a whistle and matches, his maps, and Kath's letter.

He held the still-sealed envelope in his hand as he continued examining his equipment. A magnesium striker—ought to be good for a few laughs, trying to spark kindling.

Hell, he'd done that in Boy Scouts, for christsakes. Pretty damn well too. He had a merit badge for camping, didn't he?

A couple of them. No shit.

He loved the survival hikes; just take a backpack and walk for a couple of days. What you carry is what you got. You can live off the land, if you're tough enough.

For some reason he remembered his Boy Scout days much better than the Air Force survival course he'd taken. Maybe because they had been so much fun, and the SERE had just been wet. His buddies in the Scouts would have loved a challenge like this.

Well, they would have *said* they would. Deep in enemy territory, on your own? They probably had talked about this kind of thing, not dreaming or wishing it, exactly, just kind of playing, the way kids did.

Wouldn't his friends Blitz and Beef like to get their hands on this knife? Huge, well-sharpened blade and a round pearl handle, acquired two years before at a pawnshop in Germany.

Not a pawnshop. Some sort of specialty store.

Whatever. Checklist mode. Stow memory lane and play it back later. To warm you up.

Stock taken, his next job was to move away from here. Again he contemplated firing a flare, but told himself he had to conserve them, wait until he heard something nearby. Besides, the Iraqis would be searching for at least a few more hours. Even though the flares were made so they would be difficult to see from the ground, they were not necessarily invisible, and he didn't want to do anything that might encourage the Iraqis to keep looking.

When he heard a plane or got an acknowledgment on the radio, of course, that would be different. But in the meantime, job one, item a, was to survive. And that meant being as low-key as possible.

Mongoose returned all of his equipment to its various nooks and crannies in his survival suit.

The last item was the letter.

He considered reading it, and even slid his finger to the pasted flap before stopping.

It could be bad news. Kathy could be telling him she'd found someone else and wanted a divorce.

Oh, yeah, right. Like that would really happen.

They were always good news. In the last letter, she'd written about how Robby could almost say "daddy."

Not bad for a three-month-old.

He was almost four months now. Mongoose didn't feel a picture in the envelope, but you never knew unless you opened it.

A picture would keep him going.

Mongoose slipped his finger under the side of the paper. It was one of those tissue-thin jobs, where the writing paper folds up to become the envelope.

He'd feel a photo, and there wasn't one here. If he opened the letter, it would be impossible to keep from reading it.

He ought to ration it like the water, spread it out so it would last. Read a few lines, then stop.

No way he could do that. It wasn't like stopping at just one water packet. He would read one sentence and his eyes would automatically grope for the next. And then the next. He'd have to use his flashlight, and it would take five, ten, fifteen minutes.

He had to get going. This was the first place the Iraqis would look if they came for him.

Better to save the letter. A treat, make it. When he really felt down and couldn't go on.

Carefully, he folded the envelope in half and then half again. He kept it in his hand as he started to walk from the small copse, kept it between his fingers for a long time before finally tucking it away.

PART TWO

HOME FRONT

24

Ordinarily, Robby took a nap now. Kathy Johnson counted on it; she used the hour-long break from her infant son to take a shower and, sometimes, to sneak a cigarette on her mother-in-law's porch. It wasn't like she had to sneak out to smoke exactly, but she'd made such a big thing about giving cigarettes up during her pregnancy that she felt she'd be letting people down if they knew she had gone back. And as welcoming as her husband's parents were toward her and the baby, they were still parents. It was an odd feeling, now that she was a parent herself.

But today Robby didn't seem to want to nap. He was nearly four months old, born only a few weeks before her husband had gotten the news that he was leaving for the Gulf. She tried rocking him and singing; when that didn't work Kathy gave him her breast again, swaying gently in the overstuffed old chair in their room as she tried to feed and rock him to sleep. Finally, his eyes stayed closed. She waited until his arms went limp before getting up slowly and gently placing him inside the crib.

Stepping back, she suddenly felt very cold, as if wrapped

in ice. She began to shudder. Her mother-in-law kept the thermostat at seventy-two degrees, and had double-insulated panes behind the storm windows, but Kathy felt the chill deep in her bones. She stood shivering for nearly a minute before it passed, and kept her arms wrapped tightly around her as she tiptoed from the room and headed down the hall toward the bathroom.

She had just started the water when the phone rang. She and the baby were alone in the house; there was an answering machine, but she was afraid the noise would wake Robby and she rushed to take the call, even though it meant going all the way downstairs to the kitchen in only her robe.

Her brother Peter's voice leapt from the receiver.

"Kathy?"

"Peter?"

"Go turn on CNN."

She knew then. The shudder she had felt a few minutes before returned with a fury; her body trembled so hard her robe fell open.

"Kath? I'll stay on the line. Just turn on the TV."

The phone was cordless. Kathy carried it with her as she walked through the smallish Cape Cod to the living room as deliberately as she could manage.

Though she'd been here for weeks, she still hadn't mastered the cable layout and the remote control. The screen flashed with a picture of a talk show host cajoling some guest into accepting a fashion makeover. Kathy had to go through channel by channel until finally the all-news network appeared.

Two men were talking. She thought she recognized the man on the right, a retired Air Force officer, though she couldn't decide whether it was because she had actually seen him before on the channel or because he had a generic, bland sort of face.

They flashed up a picture of an A-10A Thunderbolt II, the plane her husband flew, the plane he and the other pilots called the Warthog, or simply, "Hog."

She waited for the rest. There was a map of Saudi Arabia and Iraq. An air base supposedly used by the Hogs was marked out near the Gulf on the Saudi side of the border. She realized that the location of the air base was incorrect, though she wasn't sure whether it was a mistake or something done deliberately so the Iraqis wouldn't know where the Hogs were.

She knew it was supposed to be Jimmy's base. All the Hogs flew from the same one.

"Kathy?"

She looked at the phone in her hand, unsure how it had gotten there.

"Kath? Are you still there? I hear the TV."

She stared down at the worn, golden tufts of the freshly washed carpet, her eyes trailing slowly around the perfectly kept living room and its carefully arranged knickknacks and icons, the photographs of the Johnsons' three sons and two wives and their three, now four grandchildren, the souvenir from Disney World and the trophy that Jimmy had won for graduating second in his class and a medal that had been presented to his younger brother during an amateur olympics competition three years ago and a photo in a pewter frame of the entire Johnson clan last summer at a picnic. Her eyes caught her just-rounding belly, then the apprehension clearly marked on her face. Finally her eyes slipped over to her husband, so proud next to her, so ready to be a father after all these years of trying, so into it, having read every book as if having a child was like reading instruction manuals on a new kind of airplane. He was in his shorts and yes, he had nice legs, with sharp, thick muscles. His chest and arms were well-sculpted too, but she'd always liked his legs and his eyes the best.

"Kathy?"

And finally, she returned her attention to the television screen, where another photo of her husband was being shown, a still from a video clip apparently taken a day or two earlier by coincidence. Beneath the scratchy frame were the words "Believed down in Iraq."

25

Sergeant Clyston had just entered the building when he saw his colonel charge through the hallway from the squadron room into his office. The door flew open and slammed shut; almost immediately there was a loud roar as Colonel Knowlington barked at some hapless military operator to get him a so-and-so-and-so-and-so line to such-and-such in Riyadh, and so-and-so now.

Clyston hadn't seen the colonel like this in a long, long time—in fact, he couldn't remember him ever being this pissed off. He realized that it must have to do with Mongoose, but couldn't quite figure out what would have sent Knowlington ballistic.

The chief master sergeant eased his 267 pounds gingerly down the hallway as the tirade reached new heights.

"Who the fuck gave out the fucking information!" the colonel shouted. "What the hell were they thinking? Using his name! Get me that scumbag because I am going to tear him three new fucking assholes! Johnson has a goddamn wife and a little fucking baby. Shitting hell."

The stream of curses continued unabated for at least five minutes. Clyston felt himself shudder when the colonel hung up the phone. It had been a long time since anything Knowlington did scared him. Hell, it had been eons since *anything* scared him. But here he was, graybeard and all, standing in the hallway and feeling not a little like a newbie private on his first assignment. He actually knocked on the door.

"Who is it?"

"It's me. Sergeant Clyston."

"Come," snapped Knowlington.

"Colonel?"

"Allen. What the fuck's up? You hear this bullshit?"

"Major Johnson being shot down?"

"It's on fucking CNN. Every fucking detail."

"CNN?"

"Some douche-bag with his head up his ass talked to the fucking network! I can't fucking believe it. They confirmed his name and everything. They could just as well have given the fucking Iraqis a map. Wait until I find out who it was. Just wait."

There was little doubt in Clyston's mind that his boss would tear the person in two, no matter what his or her rank was—even if it had been the President himself. Knowlington wasn't a particularly big man, but at the moment he looked like he could wipe the floor with Mike Tyson.

"Well, what the fuck's up?" the colonel demanded.

"I wanted you to know that Devil Three has a clean bill of health," said Clyston. "And the rest of the squadron is primed and ready, so you're not going to need any backups sitting back here in the hangars. They can take off at first light. Sooner, if you want."

Knowlington's heart rate descended to merely apocalyptic levels. "You read my mind," he said.

"I thought you'd want us in the mix."

Knowlington nodded. He was staring beyond the sergeant, as if he could see through the walls all the way to Iraq. "I hate those motherfucking newspeople, Allen," he said finally. "They screwed us in Nam. Man, they screwed us bad."

The sergeant gave him an all-purpose "yup." This wasn't Vietnam, though he wasn't about to point that out. He also had a somewhat different view of the media—in his opinion, it was the brass and politicians who had fucked up; a lot of the newspeople who weren't jerks were just trying to show how it was from a grunt's eye view. Nothing wrong with that. But Skull had personal reasons for his interpretation, and the Capo respected that.

"I got to find Goose's wife's phone number," Knowlington told him.

"You're going to call her?"

"Wouldn't you?"

"Wouldn't, uh, wouldn't be my place."

"Yeah, well, I have to take care of this myself. She's probably watching the fucking television right now. Jesus H. Christ. Do me a favor, would you? Shotgun stayed north to try and help the search. He hadn't gotten back to King Khalid last time I checked. Find Wong and tell him I want to talk to Shotgun as soon as he lands there. Tell him I don't care if he has to go up to KKMC himself and lasso him, I want to be talking to him within the hour."

"Wong?"

"Yeah. He's got a screwy sense of humor but he's exactly the kind of guy you can count on in the clutch with something like this. Got those intel and Pentagon connections. Wong's okay."

Clyston nodded.

"How's the crew taking it?" Knowlington asked.

"Everybody wants to do what they can to get him back."

"You tell them we're bringing him back if I have to fucking hike up to Baghdad myself and carry him out on my back."

"Yourself?"

"Yeah. Me."

"This mission approved by Black Hole?"

"You know, Sergeant, with all due respect, I can't remember making you officer of the day, let alone director of operations."

"Yes, sir."

"What?"

"Nothing."

Knowlington's frown and silence indicated he expected

the Capo to tell him what was on his mind, no matter whether it was something he wanted to hear or not.

"Well, uh, taking the mission yourself," Clyston told him.

"You think I'm too old?"

"No. You're just, you're getting a little excited. Usually, you're ice."

"Yeah, well, I'm pissed. The CNN crapola. I'll calm down, enough to nail these fuckers anyway."

"You sound like Shotgun," Clyston told him.

Knowlington didn't answer. His eyes were back in their far-away stare.

The colonel actually sounded like another pilot Clyston had known—*Captain* Knowlington, Thud and Phantom pilot extraordinaire. The captain had been a hell of a stick man, a balls-out jock as lucky as he was skilled and smarter than both. That wasn't a combination you found in a lot of officers.

Brash as all hell, though; forgot to use his smarts and got himself into situations where he needed every ounce of that skill and more than his share of luck.

Clyston liked Captain Knowlington, admired the hell out of him. Captain Knowlington had balls the size of watermelons and a will to match. But even back in Vietnam, the sergeant had had enough experience to know that that wasn't the sort of man who should command a fighter squadron, even during a war. He was too hotheaded, too quick to react, too close to the situation to think slowly and carefully. Leading by impulse got a lot of people killed.

Colonel Knowlington had his faults, but Colonel Knowlington was one hell of a boss. Saying he was like ice didn't cover a quarter of it. Hell, he was as cold and calculating as a goddamn computer, and twice as smart. And he not only cared about his people, but trusted them to do their jobs without his hand on their shoulders. He even asked NCOs what they thought—and admitted taking their advice once in a while.

Since coming to Saudi Arabia, Knowlington had somehow gotten beyond the booze and doubts that had dogged him for years. Something had clicked, and all his experience and the better parts of his personality had just fallen into place. Maybe the war had brought out the best in him.

They needed Colonel Knowlington to lead the squadron, not Captain Knowlington. Cold, well-thought-out decisions that would keep everyone alive while still doing maximum hurt to Saddam. Morale-boosting respect for even the lowest airman, respect that was genuine, not bullshit, the kind of thing that got a homesick nineteen-year-old out of his tent in the morning determined to check every bolt twice just because the old man was counting on him.

But there was no way to talk about that now.

Damn—was he kidding about flying north himself?

"Something else?" Skull asked.

"Not that I can think of," Clyston told him. "I'll see if I can find Captain Wong for you."

Knowlington didn't bother answering, already reaching for the phone on his desk.

26

The Hog was moving a bit too fast for a picture-perfect landing, but Shotgun didn't particularly care. He jerked the poor plane onto the concrete with an uncharacteristic screech, annoyed that he had to come down at all. He'd left the area where Mongoose had been hit with only the greatest reluctance. Even if he couldn't see anything, he felt he belonged nearby.

True, the Air Force had different jobs for different people, and for all he knew as he began taxiing at the end of the airstrip, a division of Special Forces troops were carrying Goose back home on their freakin' shoulders right now. The point was, he ought to be there. Hog pilots looked after their own. He was the guy's freakin' wingman, and it was half or maybe three-quarters his fault he'd gone down in the first place.

Maybe not, but it was the principle of the thing.

Shotgun told this in so many words to the airman who was waving the Hog off the landing strip to make way for other planes. Fortunately for the airman, he was several yards away, outside the aircraft, and wearing ear protection.

"What I'm talking about here," Shotgun shouted as he

moved toward a refitting area, banging on his canopy, "is getting refueled like yesterday. And I need the cannon reloaded. You with me? I'm thinking we can rig an extra set of landing lights, maybe put together some sort of lens that'll make them into searchlights. That's what I'm talking about. Ten minutes' worth of work. What I'm talking about is smoking any Iraqi that comes within ten miles of him. Can't be smoking anybody with no bullets. You're showing me to a candy man, right? To get some new iron? I don't see no dragon down there and I can use some new bullets in the cannon. Hey, kid, you listening to me?"

The jerry-rigged-landing-light idea had occurred to him as he flew back to base. It wasn't a bad idea, except for the fact that it would alert every Iraqi within a hundred miles that he was coming. Sure, the Hog could take a lot of abuse, but the rescue helicopters might catch some of the flak too. The Iraqis were notoriously bad shots.

What he needed was a pair of Maverick Gs—the enhanced air-to-ground missiles had an excellent infrared seeker that could be pressed into service as night-vision equipment. A squadron had been practicing the technique for weeks.

And if he could find an Army Apache pilot, he'd really strike gold. The Apache drivers had kick-ass night goggles. Worked off the reflected light from the stars and the moon. Have to adapt them a bit for a Hog, but shit, what would that take? A little fiddling with a screwdriver? Some duct tape to completely black out the Hog cockpit, or create a little shade to see through? War was about experimentation.

How would he get an Apache pilot to give up his glasses? Poor shit would probably have to pay for them out of his own pocket.

Maybe a swap—he could trade his customized Colt, a very serious personally modified .45, the kind of gun a real Army guy ought to salivate over, for a mere temporary loan. Have the glasses back before sunup, no harm done. Say they were misplaced or in the shop if anyone asks.

Hell, he'd even throw in a couple of Twinkies.

No self-respecting member of the U.S. Army could refuse such a deal. His plan set, Shotgun shuttled into a parking area a few hundred yards from the end of the runway. He was disappointed—no choppers in sight.

He was just checking his gas gauges to see if he might somehow persuade the fumes to take him a bit further when an Army officer ran toward the front of the plane, waving his arms like a jumping jack. The man made a motion as if he wanted him to cut his engines.

Shotgun leaned his large body out the side of the plane to see if the officer could direct him to the nearest Apache.

"Cut your engines and crank down your ladder!" shouted the man.

He was definitely Army. You could tell by the overly serious expression on his face.

And the fact that he kept his distance from the airplane. In Shotgun's experience, the overwhelming majority of Army officers were afraid of flying. Otherwise they would have joined the Air Force.

"I said, where can I find an Apache?" Shotgut shouted.

"Cut your engines and crank down your ladder," repeated the officer, motioning with his hand to make Shotgun understand.

Since it was designed to work from front-line bases with minimal amenities, the A-10A was equipped with its own ladder, which the pilot could operate from the cockpit. Shotgun cut his motors and complied, though unwinding the ladder felt a bit too much like putting down an anchor, under the circumstances.

A flush-red face belonging to an Army major quickly appeared over the side.

"Why the hell didn't you shut your engines when I told you to?" the officer asked.

"When did you tell me to shut off the engines?"

"You couldn't see me?"

"Saw you just now," said Shotgun, who had decided to be on his best behavior. "Can you direct me to the Apache pilots? There's a Twinkie in it for you. A little crushed, I apologize, but definitely edible."

"Are you Captain O'Rourke or not?"

"I was this morning."

"Look, I don't have time for bullshit. We've just been put

on a goddamn Scud alert. You got to get chem gear on and get this plane secured. Then you call your squadron commander."

"Who?"

"Call your colonel. But before that, get yourself into protective gear."

"My best protection's a fully loaded Hog," Shotgun told him. "Shit, I got Sidewinders—I'll nail the damn missiles while they're inbound."

The major grumbled something concerning the sanity of Air Force personnel and disappeared back down the ladder.

"Colonel wants to talk to you," said Captain Wong when Shotgun finally got a connection to the home drome.

"Yeah, well I want to talk to him."

"Okay."

"So put him on."

"I don't know where he is."

"Well, I sure as shit don't."

"Wait, I'll look in his office."

Shotgun pushed himself back in the field chair. Wong was one of those absent-minded-professor types. Guy had a shitload of knowledge about Russian-made air defenses; he was supposedly the world expert, and had figured out some fairly tricky stuff for Devil Squadron since coming from Black Hole the first day of the war. But he couldn't put mustard on a bologna and cheese sandwich without detailed instructions.

Bologna and cheese sure as hell would hit the spot right about now. Better: the double Big Mac with extra-large fries and strawberry shake that was undoubtedly sitting in his tent at the home drome.

Amazing where Fed Ex could deliver.

As forward air strips went, KKMC wasn't particularly spartan, but it did lack a full-service McDonald's. Still, there were enough Army guys floating around. Hog crews pitted here all the time. That much creativity around demanded a bit more research on his part; there might be a fast-food outlet somewhere around here. In fact, now that he thought about it, the round-domed building nearby would be the perfect place for the local Dunkin' Donuts franchise: If you squinted just right it kind of looked like an upside-down coffee cup.

Super-size Dunkin' Donuts coffee and two, no, make that three Boston cremes, would definitely charge him up for the return trip north. Chocolate a little gooey on the top, just enough to leave his fingertips covered with lickable creme.

"Shotgun, where the fuck are you?"

"Hey, good evening to you too, Colonel."

"What the hell are you doing at KKMC?"

"Getting more bullets in case I see any rattlesnakes up north."

Knowlington grunted. Shotgun didn't know the commander too well, but Knowlington came with a reputation; he'd kicked serious butt flying over Vietnam and he didn't dick his pilots around. So when the colonel asked if he'd seen a parachute, Shotgun didn't hedge.

"I thought I saw something, but now I'm not even sure of that. I found the wreckage but couldn't see the seat or the chute anywhere. And I looked."

"And no beacon?"

"I'm thinking the radio screwed up. Got to be. Probably a transistor blew or something."

"The backup too?"

It was a comment not a question, so Shutgun didn't answer. He could tell that the colonel, unlike the intel guys he'd spoken to after parking the plane, knew Mongoose was still alive down there—it was just a question of coming up with a plan to get him back.

"I got this idea," Shotgun told him. "If I had some Maverick Gs, I could go back and scan the ground. Hell, the eyes in those things are better than an owl's. Problem is, I can't seem to drum up any up here. The one sergeant who seems to know what the hell I'm talking about bitches about how expensive they are and claims all of the missiles are at Fahd. I don't know if it's true, but I haven't seen any myself."

"I doubt they're sensitive enough to pick him up, even in the desert."

For just a second, Shotgun's faith in his commander wavered.

"We can't just leave him up there, Colonel."

"I'm not leaving him up there," snapped Knowlington. "I'm fucking thinking."

"Yes, sir. Sorry, sir."

Had Shotgun thought about it, he would have realized it was perhaps the first time he had used the word "sir" in Saudi Arabia—and undoubtedly the first time he had ever used it in two consecutive sentences since training. He hung on the line through a long silence, waiting while Knowlington worked the thing through in his head.

"All right. Go catch some rest," said the colonel finally. "I have a few things to get around down here. I'll be up with the Mavericks three hours before dawn, latest. That gives you a little time for a catnap."

"You're trucking them up?"

"I'm flying, you asshole. You and I are going to find Mongoose, assuming the Special Ops boys haven't picked him up by then. You have a problem with that?"

"No, sir. Shit, no."

"Well, then get some fucking sleep. I don't want a zombie watching my six."

"Yes, sir."

Shotgun looked at the handset as the line clicked dead. The old man hadn't flown a combat mission since he'd come to Saudi Arabia. The word was that Skull Knowlington, who'd originally been assigned to head a squadron that existed only on paper, had maybe a hundred hours in the Hog cockpit, or some ridiculously low amount.

But hell. Knowlington was a goddamn legend. If anybody could find Mongoose—anyone besides Shotgun, that is— *he* could.

"Fuckin' A," the pilot said. "I think."

27

Mongoose aimed the small strobe unit in the direction of the sound. He had already fired a pencil flare to get their attention, and now hoped the strobe would direct whoever was up there to his location.

The strobe's light was hooded, making it difficult to see on the ground. In theory anyway. He couldn't worry about any of that now; he kept strobing, hoping to hear the engine again. The radio was pumping out its own emergency beacon.

But the plane was no longer nearby. He made a voice broadcast; when there was no answer he fired another mini-flare. As the rocket arced upwards, he tried the radio again. Mongoose swung the dial back and forth, from beacon to voice, radioing his distress call.

"I'll take a pizza with anchovies to go," he added at the end.

Whatever he'd heard was gone. He settled back against the stones he'd lined up as a small shelter. He'd dug out some of the ground with his boot, like a small foxhole. It had been something to do, to take his mind off how stinking cold he was.

The radio was probably busted. That wasn't particularly lucky.

Might've broken somehow when he landed. Or it was just one of those dumb, stupid things.

There was another one back in the seat pack.

But where the hell was that now? Could he trace his way back in the dark and the slowly lifting fog?

He heard a noise in the distance, this time on the ground.

Was it really there? His ears buzzed with something, but it didn't seem real. Slowly, as deliberately as possible, he slid the strobe light back into a vest pocket and removed his pistol from its holster.

He stayed like that, gun just in front of his chest, for a long time. The noise grew louder, then faded. It was definitely a truck, and far off. His eyes ached, filtering the darkness for the head beams or taillights, but they didn't appear. The moon, a dull crescent, drifted through some clouds, cold and distant.

When he was in Boy Scouts, they used to tell ghost stories about kids so lost in the wilderness they turned into walking skeletons, haunting the woods for centuries. He thought of those stories now as he crouched back into his small, safe place and reholstered his pistol.

The stories had scared the piss out of him. He remembered being so afraid that he wouldn't get out of his sleeping bag to take a leak. Instead, he'd lie awake all night, waiting for dawn.

That was as a second-class Scout, still pretty green, his first full year as a Scout. The next summer, at the wilderness camp in the Adirondacks, now Star rank, he laughed at the stories, told a lot of them himself, and took a leak whenever he damn well pleased.

He was still a little scared actually, but no way would he let on, even to himself.

His days as a Scout were all flooding back. He remembered one of his toughest tests—to join one of the Scouts' "secret" lodges, he'd had to endure an initiation that consisted of being left alone in the wilderness with only a map and compass. He was given two hours to get back to camp.

He'd hurt his knee a few days before, and soon after he started he slipped down a ravine and twisted it pretty bad. Mongoose knew from one of his friends that older Scouts monitored an initiate carefully; they were always within shouting distance in case something went wrong.

He could have called out. His injury would have been considered a mitigating factor and he would have probably been given another chance at the initiation. But he didn't. Instead he hobbled on down the mountain, finding a stick to use as a crutch and showing up at camp nearly six hours later, well past the deadline. When the lodge elder—that was what they called the leader—asked why he was so late, Mongoose just shrugged. He'd thrown away the stick before coming into camp, and refused to let his knee be an excuse. He told the others he'd failed the initiation because he had taken too much time hiking in.

A few days later, the kids in the lodge "kidnapped" him from his tent, and made him a member anyway. They all knew what had happened, even though he didn't tell anyone.

That was one of the proudest moments of his life. Even now. It compared to the first day he'd flown a jet fighter alone, and the day his son was born—actually the day after, when he was telling everyone he knew, because the day it happened was too consuming to feel anything but the moment.

In some ways, the initiation was his most difficult accomplishment. It would have been so easy to make excuses.

Another day strayed into his memory, a snatch of a day. He had his father's car and hit another car in a parking lot, broke the taillight.

He'd gotten out, inspected the cars. There was no damage to his. The other car was a relatively new Chrysler.

He hopped back into his dad's car and took off.

Coward.

Mongoose kicked himself for doing that, as if it had happened this morning instead of thirteen or fourteen years before. That wasn't him—he was the kid who hiked down the mountain on a makeshift crutch, and refused to make excuses. He should have left a note on the guy's windshield, offered to make good, whatever the consequences.

Plenty of times he had. But the car came back at him now. He pushed down against the ground, kicked out some more dirt in his miniature bunker, felt his knee tweak a bit.

Scouting was a good time. The best camping was during the winter, when you literally froze your tush off just taking a dump. He almost never managed more than an hour or two sleeping at night, even when they stayed in cabins. He was always so tired he'd sleep the entire day when he got home.

It felt colder than that now, and it was going to get even worse. He rubbed his arms against his chest, moved around a bit, stood, and walked a little.

He wanted Robby to go into Boy Scouts, assuming they still existed. Assuming they'd let him join with his father in the service. Military life being what it was, it could be hard to join an organization. But plenty of kids did.

Tough as hell to raise a family when you were gone fighting a war. To be away when they needed you, when your wife needed you . . .

He caught himself, got back into checklist mode.

A good radio was essential. He could walk back to the trees, then find his way to the pack from there. He'd use the road as much as he dared; find it from the trees, then walk parallel until he came to the wadi. From there it would be easy to get back to the seat.

First, though, there might be a way to fix the radio he had. Shake it, at least—nothing wrong with banging something to make it work, Shotgun used to say.

Good old Shotgun. He'd be busting an artery looking for him.

If he was still alive. More than likely he was in worse shape. Maybe hadn't even gotten out alive.

And it was Mongoose's fault. He'd taken the planes low to smoke the Scuds, even though it was dangerous and against all sorts of cautions and orders and common sense.

Not Hog sense, but that wasn't the same thing.

Mongoose took the radio in one hand and gripped the gun by the barrel. Not exactly something a technician might approve of, but what the hell—he banged them together, then tried another quick broadcast.

When he heard nothing, he put the radio away and began walking.

28

It wasn't until after Dixon had told Colonel Knowlington
about Mongoose that he felt the true depth of his uselessness
here. It wasn't as if he expected to be tasked to fly up there
and bring him back—in fact, the air tasking order had
already given the Devil Squadron a heavy agenda; there
probably was no room in the frag for anything like that, and
other units were already assigned search-and-rescue duty
anyway. But there was no question that Dixon was far from
the action, a million miles from where he belonged.

Dixon finished up his work, then checked around to see
if anything new had come in on Major Johnson's flight.

Nothing. Not a good sign. But there was nothing he could
do about it, sitting in his Riyadh cubbyhole. Reluctantly, he
decided to keep his dinner date with an American family in
a "guest" development not far from the center of the city. He
hoped real food might take his mind off his uselessness for
a few hours.

Thanks partly to their great oil wealth, the Saudis used a
large number of foreigners to help run their country. Many
of the workers were domestics and drudges from poor
countries such as Pakistan. But there was also a fair number

of highly skilled workers, including Westerners. Most lived apart from the rest of Saudi society, their "hosts" not wanting to risk the contamination of Western mores in a Muslim culture. His new acquaintances—cousins of an Air Force officer he'd gone through training with—lived in one such compound, a kind of gilded ghetto where, for the most part, Islamic strictures such as those about women's dress and alcohol could be safely ignored.

But that didn't explain why his friend greeted him at the front door in a full-body chem suit.

"You're late. Where's your protective gear?"

"Do I have the right house?" asked Dixon.

"It's me, Fernandez," said the man through the suit. "I've been waiting for you. Come in. We're on Scud alert. Everyone else is in the shelter."

"Shelter?"

"It's not really a shelter, but it will do as long as there's not a direct hit. The walls are reinforced and it's airtight. We have an air exchanger, but I don't trust it. Where's your suit?"

"I don't have one."

"What? Well, come on, we'll get you a mask at least. Come on."

Like a lot of other guys in Saudi Arabia, Dixon didn't take the chemical warfare threat very seriously. Nor did he think much of the Scuds, which were annoying but not particularly accurate.

Though maybe that ought to worry him a bit.

Inside the hallway, Dixon had to duck around a crystal chandelier that looked like it belonged in an opera house. They walked through the public part of the sprawling one-level house, past a luxurious, Western-style living room and a dining room that could have been in a palace somewhere, down a second hallway into a back room.

"I know the place looks pretty drab. We've packed away the valuables," said Fernandez through his hood. He worked as an accountant for a Saudi oil concern owned by a member of the royal family. "I know what you're thinking—we don't have a proper basement. But this wing was supposedly steel-reinforced. I don't know whether to believe them or not. But at least there's no windows."

They stepped down a single step and continued through yet another hallway, this one lined with expensive-looking paintings. Dixon wondered what the stuff that had been packed away looked like.

His nose twitched with the smell of roast beef. Before he could ask about it, his host opened the door at the very end of the hall, revealing a thick piece of plastic. He reached down and pulled it up. A dozen people, all wearing gas masks or protective hoods, a few in full chem suits, crowded around a brown leather love seat and ottoman in the large room, watching a CNN feed. A correspondent in a chem suit but no hood was speaking to the camera in hushed tones.

"Here's a whole suit," said Fernandez, leading him to a table in the corner. He held up a suit that was clearly too small for Dixon's frame.

"It's not going to fit."

"Take the mask then. Like I said, I don't trust the equipment."

"I honestly don't think it's necessary."

His host's answer was cut off by the peal of a siren. As loud as the siren was, the explosion that followed was even louder.

Dixon quickly began stuffing himself into the gear.

29

Of Colonel Knowlington's many friends in the Pentagon, Alex Sherman was among the least sympathetic. For one thing, Sherman was a civilian; he didn't quite understand the wrenches your guts went through when people shot at you.

For another, Sherman was a reformed alcoholic; he took a tough-love stance toward everybody and everything, Michael Knowlington especially. They'd met each other in Saigon, well before either had admitted drinking was a problem, let alone something they ought to give up. Sherman was the one media person Skull could stand. Actually, he was a PR consultant, then for the Army, now for the Joint Chiefs, with a title nearly as long as Knowlington's service record. Sherman's opinion of reporters was every bit as jaded, though far more nuanced than the colonel's; having fed the sharks for so long, he'd come to understand and maybe like a few.

Which was one reason Skull let him have it full blast for the CNN story.

"Hey, you through? It's not like I'm the assignment editor, or the guy with the big mouth," said Sherman. "It's just one of those things, Mikey. A reporter happened to be around when some guys were talking."

"One of those things? I thought there were fucking censors to keep the lid on."

"Yeah, well, somebody's butt'll fry on that, believe me."

"These goddamn bozos are going to get him killed."

"That's not true. If anything, this may help keep him alive. If Saddam knows we know he's alive, the odds for survival are better."

"You have statistics on that?"

"Believe me, we're just as peed over here as you are."

"Has anyone talked to his wife yet?"

"Well, by now—"

"I haven't been able to get a line through to her. Can you arrange that for me?"

"Me?"

"You have some pull, don't you?"

"I don't know if I can get approval, for one thing."

"Screw approval. Just get me the phone number. We don't have it for some reason, and it's unlisted."

"Mikey, you really think you should talk to her? What the hell are you going to say?"

"You going to help me or what?"

Sherman's long sigh announced surrender. "Let me see what I can do."

"I'll stay on the line."

"Come on."

"I may never be able to get you again."

"Jesus."

Knowlington leaned back from his desk and saw that Captain Wong was standing uncomfortably in the doorway. "Those Mavericks on the plane?" he asked the major.

"Begging your pardon, sir, but for the record, I'm not a spear carrier."

As pissed as he was, Knowlington just had to laugh. "Owww—that's a bad pun. Sometimes you have to give it rest, though, Wong. So, they're on?"

"They're placing two on the plane as we speak. Colonel, can we discuss my transfer? I'd rather be studying Russian invoices for rivets than dealing with ad hoc, unvetted combat plans that rely on outmoded weapons pushed beyond their technical capabilities into non-functional paradigms of non-optimum performance. Sir."

"God, Wong, sometimes your jokes go over even my head. Anybody else, I'd think they were serious. Shit, you crack me up, you know that?"

"I am serious," Wong said.

"Thanks. Listen, go get some rest. I appreciate your schlepping around this stuff for me. Really. And your humor."

"I wasn't making a joke."

"Go on, get out of here."

Knowlington waved him away with a laugh. Damned best straight man in the Air Force. It was the face that did it—so damn serious, it set everything else up.

Non-functional paradigms—what a ball-buster. No wonder they had kicked him out of Black Hole.

Truth was, Knowlington knew that using the missiles' infrared seeker to look for a man on the outskirts of the desert was like using a metal detector to find a bullet in a gravel pit at twenty thousand feet. But they had to do something.

Truth was, the fact that no one had picked up Mongoose's radio beacon meant that maybe there was nothing to be done. But Knowlington wasn't ready to accept that.

"Hey, you still on the line or what?"

"Yeah, I'm here," Knowlington told his friend. He stood up in his chair, mouth suddenly dry. The colonel ran his free hand back over his forehead, then down his chin and neck.

"Okay," Sherman said, apparently to an operator. "It's yours from here, Mikey. And you're welcome."

"Hello?" said a woman's voice, soft and bewildered.

To the colonel, it sounded a lot like one of his sisters. They were, after all, the reason he'd wanted to call. Both had been contacted two different times by the Air Force, once because his plane turned up missing and once when he was actually shot down. He wasn't sure now whether there had been phone calls or someone in person coming to the house; he just knew they had talked to someone.

The time he was missing had been a first-class screwup all around. They had him dead. But his sisters told him later it was better knowing that someone was at least making an attempt to contact them and knew who they were. Being in the dark was the worst thing; it made you feel farther away than you really were.

"Hello?"

"Is this Kathleen Johnson, Major James Johnson's wife?"

"Who is this?"

A sliver of steel came into her voice, resolution or stoicism, or maybe even anger.

"Kathleen, this is Colonel Knowlington. Your husband's commander."

"Oh."

"This isn't an official call. I wanted to talk to you personally and tell you I was sorry about the television broadcast. That was a mistake."

"The Pentagon people said they weren't sure how it got out. They already apologized. So did one of the Air Force officers who called to say they were on their way."

Well, at least someone there was on the ball, Skull thought to himself.

Then he thought, shit. But it was too late not to talk to her.

"I wanted to tell you that we're doing everything we can to pick him up."

"He is still alive, isn't he?"

Knowlington fought back the impulse to assure her that her husband was fine. It was natural and human, but it wasn't fair.

"I have to be honest, Kathleen. We're working on that. We've spotted the wreckage and he's not there."

"You're sure he ejected?"

Again, he squelched the impulse to lie. "We believe he did. But we have not had confirmation."

"I see."

Her voice had become small again. He could hear crying in the background: their child.

"I'm sorry, Colonel, but I have to go. Thank you for calling."

Knowlington put the phone down and sat at his desk a moment longer, his eyes staring at the blank, smooth top. Was it better to be honest, or was it just cruel?

30

Sergeant Clyston sank into his Stratolounger, luxuriating in the thick richness of the Mozart pumping through his earphones. Don Giovanni was just now being handed the Devil's bill for his incredible success with women. It was a moment that never failed to please the Capo, rating right up there with the time he had figured out how to knock an entire hour off the overhaul of a GE J79–15 turbojet.

Clyston's appreciation of justice and its musical expression was not unalloyed, however; the sergeant had escaped to his highly customized temp tent to contemplate a serious moral question: Should he let Skull fly in combat?

In theory and in law, Colonel Knowlington outranked the sergeant by a country mile, and could command himself to do anything he pleased. But theory and law did not apply to the Capo di Capo; or rather, they did, but in a way considerably more convoluted than might be laid out in a military handbook.

Any good crew chief feels responsible not only for his airplane but his pilot. Clyston was no different, and in fact as he got older had become something of a father figure to several of the pilots to whom he'd "loaned" his planes. His role was an advisor, though, not a boss; he worked with the officers entirely by suggestion, though admittedly some suggestions were stronger and more strategically placed than others. Shortly after coming to Saudi Arabia, one such suggestion had grounded a suicidal pilot. That was an extreme example, of course; to a man the squadron's pilots had abilities and "stuff" that even a graybeard like Clyston could admire.

His concern about the colonel went beyond both his normal concern for a pilot and his ancient friendship with the commander. As the squadron's top NCO, he had the squadron to consider.

Skull wasn't drinking anymore; Clyston knew that for a fact. The snap was back in his walk, and his judgment was right on. Hell, even drinking, the guy made a lot of right moves, if only because he gave his subordinates nearly free reign.

But flying was different. Flying in the dark, miles and miles behind the lines, pushing the plane to do something it wasn't designed to do?

At his peak, there were few pilots in the Air Force better than Mikey Knowlington. But his peak had passed a long time ago. He'd put in some large hours over the past few weeks, and done the flight test on the Hog today without a problem, but no one was shooting at him.

Thing was, even if it wasn't Knowlington flying, going north wasn't a particularly smart thing to do. Get into trouble and butts were going to be fried.

Where would the 535th be if Skull's ass was the one getting burnt?

Worse, what if he was cooked by the same SOB who took down Mongoose? The major could be a class-one anal prick, but he was a kick-butt flier with high time in the Hog cockpit. Whoever got him wasn't just lucky, they were damn good.

Clyston was the only one in Saudi Arabia, probably the only one in the Air Force, who could talk Knowlington out of flying the mission. He was the only one who could go to Mikey and tell him, listen, you don't have to prove yourself to anybody anymore. You have to run the squadron.

Maybe he couldn't talk him out of it. This wasn't about proving he could fly combat again. This was about getting his guy back.

Especially since it was Mongoose. Clyston knew the colonel well enough to realize that, in his mind if no one else's, Skull thought he should have been the one flying that mission. He'd see getting Mongoose back as not only his job, but his duty.

Hard to talk somebody out of doing their duty.

Someone like Knowlington, it'd be impossible.

But what was Clyston's duty?

The sergeant leaned back in his chair, listening for clues as Mozart doubled back against his theme.

31

Mongoose had almost reached the trees when he heard the sound, a low, guttural moan moving in the night. At first he thought it was an animal, a wolf or hyena or something, a beast that had caught his scent and was calling its brothers for the kill.

By the time he flopped to the ground on his belly, he realized it was a truck, maybe two. The moonlight showed him the shadows moving a mile away. They felt their way toward him, slow and deliberate.

Mongoose lay on his belly, frozen by a mixture of fear and fascination, as if he were seeing someone else's nightmare. The trucks crested a small hill in the distance, kept coming.

They didn't have their headlights on. Smart precaution, but it would make it tough for them to see him here.

The shadows stopped and a beam of light erupted from the second, sweeping the ground. It found the trees, then arced slowly, still about a hundred yards away from where he lay.

That got him moving. Mongoose jumped up and began running in the opposite direction. He tripped over something, felt himself spilling forward. Somehow he managed to get his elbow out and roll with the fall. He tumbled back to his feet, ran a few more yards, saw the sweeping light from the corner of his eye, and dove once more to the ground.

The light paused on something twenty yards away. The trees maybe, or a shadow that looked like a man. Whatever it was, the trucks put their headlights on and revved their engines, moving again.

Moving toward him.

Now would be a great time for a Hog to appear. The A-10s weren't worth shit in the dark, but they would sure make him feel better.

No Hog appeared. The trucks came closer.

At most, he was a half mile from the road. Much too close. He couldn't be sure what they'd seen, but he knew he hadn't felt the light. He was still hidden. He ran ten yards, up a slight incline, then fell; rolling, he got a mouthful of grit before he managed to stop his fall.

The search beam was trained on the trees. Mongoose scrambled to his feet and started running again, hoping they would be focusing all their attention there, hoping he wasn't making too much noise. He could get over this dune or hill or whatever the hell it was and he'd be safe.

The pilot had only taken a few steps when something told him to dive for cover again; he flopped down, expecting the searchlight to play over him.

When it didn't, he turned and looked over his shoulder. One of the two trucks was now between him and the trees. Its searchlight was examining the area carefully, moving over the ground like a worm. Two long shadows blurred behind it. He saw soldiers moving like waves in the light.

Mongoose pushed back up, determined to get more distance between himself and the enemy. A machine gun opened up as he did. The hollow *pop-pop-pop* sent him back into the dirt, diving around to face them though he knew, he hoped, the bullets weren't aimed in his direction. Another gunner began firing—he realized they were automatic rifles, not machine guns; AK-47's most likely, though

Mongoose had never actually heard one off a firing range before.

There were shouts; probably the commander told the men to stop wasting their ammunition, though the pilot couldn't understand the language.

The soldiers had been spooked by the trees or something. That he could understand.

As they resumed the search, the Iraqis' shadows fluttered up from the ground, devils emerging from some ghost hole. Dark, oversized rifles loomed out at him, their barrels searching for his heart. The pilot reached for his pistol and gripped it tightly. He told himself they couldn't see him. More than likely, they would inspect the area near the road, fire a few more shots to flush him out in case he was nearby, then pile back into the trucks and go on.

Logically, he knew that was what they would do. But it didn't make it any easier to crouch here, less than a hundred yards away, listening to their grunts and the chink of their equipment as they began searching the area. They cursed loudly. One seemed to trip; again the desert exploded with small-arms fire. The searchlight swung wildly around the area; the dim edge of its shadow reached to within inches of where he had been when he first spotted them.

He had to get up over this hill. Here he was in range of their searchlight. Sooner or later, a sweep would find him.

Mongoose glanced down at the gun in his hand. Only its vague outline was visible, but he could feel it heavy and slightly moist, as if it were sweating.

It was him, not the gun. He was colder than hell and thirsty besides, but water was streaming from his pores.

If they came for him, should he fire? With surprise on his side in the dark, he could take out two or three before the others knew what was happening.

What then? Could he escape the hail of bullets that would follow?

There was another clip in his pocket. Burn the first one, reload, take them all on?

Yes, that was what he would do.

It would mean he'd die. Inevitably. The odds were stacked. There were at least a dozen shadows in the distance. Sooner or later they would find him and they wouldn't be inclined to show mercy.

Nothing in Iraq is worth dying for.

Better to be quiet, better to hide. His job was to survive. His job for Kath, and for Robby.

To survive. That was what the Air Force told him. Survive. Don't do anything stupid. You're not Rambo.

And that's an order.

But no way he could give up. Shit, that would be worse than living. Tortured, used for propaganda and God knows what.

In the dark, in the desert, they'd never find him. They might search a few yards around the trees, no more. He had to get up over that hill.

Mongoose held his breath and got up slowly, watched the shadows for a second, then began moving up the hill in a crouch-walk.

He'd gone about six feet when the Iraqis began shouting again. The search beam swung past the trees in the opposite direction.

Now was his chance.

He had just taken a step when the searchlight swung back toward him.

32

Everybody in the Air Force had their own specialty. In Shotgun's humble opinion, the candy men—the crew dogs who took care of getting bombs onto the planes—were probably the best guys at making chili. He had no theory to explain this, beyond the obvious connection with their profession. There was, at the same time, an inverse relationship between chili quality and geographical origin. Shotgun had never met a chili chef who'd been born farther south than Weston, Virginia, which was not, per se, a chili-making town. This bomb loader—Sergeant Harris P. Slocum, to be exact—was a case in point, hailing from Milwaukee. Slocum, who was happy to share his chili with an obvious connoisseur, had no explanation for it either.

The sergeant and Chevy, an airman buddy of his, had traded the chili for a pair of Shotgun's Devil Dogs, and had thrown in a can of real Coca-Cola as well. A genuine bargain, as far as Shotgun was concerned, given that the Devil Dogs were a bit mushed. The pilot was so overwhelmed by their generosity that he offered them his last Twizzler licorice sticks as well.

"You're a walking candy store, sir," said Slocum, lounging on the dragon that loaded shells into the A-10A's cannon. "So they let you fly with all this stuff in your suit?"

"Never tried to stop me. You got some more of this chili?"

"All you want, sir," said Chevy. "Hang on a second."

He trotted over to a small wheeled vehicle that usually held iron bombs, but had been pressed into duty as a kind of tool cart. The back had a pair of coolers—one with hot food, one with cold. A battery rig had been hooked up; a Mr. Coffee was just squirting water into its pot.

Shotgun thought it was damn good to see ingenuity like that so close to the front lines.

"Buddy of yours went down, huh?" Slocum asked.

"Yeah. I got a bead on him, though. We'll pick him up before the sun comes up."

"Tough country up there."

Shotgun shrugged. Chevy returned with a fresh cup of chili. It wasn't a cup exactly—they used old cans as containers. You had to make sacrifices due to the war and all.

"What's it like to get shot at?" Slocum asked.

"Shot at?" Shotgun took a mouthful of the chili. Maybe it could have used another hit of cayenne. "Nothing really. Hadn't thought about it."

"You don't think about it?" asked Chevy.

"Nah. Mostly what you think about is, how can I wax that son of a bitch for having the balls to try to shoot me? That's what you think about. That and maybe, I should've had the Boss on instead of Nirvana."

"The Boss?" asked Chevy.

"Bruce Springsteen. You guys never heard of Springsteen?"

"Well, uh, sure we did, sir," said Slocum. "But, uh, you listen to music while you're flying?"

"Doesn't everybody?" Shotgun got up and showed them his customized Walkman hookup, which he had wired into his suit. They whistled in admiration. "Nothing like listening to 'E Street Shuffle' while you're pounding Saddam's pissants. You figure that coffee's ready now?"

• • • •

His stomach full and thermos loaded with coffee—a little weak, but no sense complaining—Shotgun did a careful preflight of his Hog. The plane's stores had been reloaded; its gas tanks were now filled to the brim. Four Rockeye II cluster bombs had been slapped onto the hardpoints. The big drum that fed the cannon was packed with bullets, and Shotgun had even managed to scrounge a few plastic-wrapped generic-brand cupcakes to refurbish his survival pantry.

Moving from front to back, Shotgun checked over the plane carefully. He ran his hands across the wings and ailerons, feeling the metal. The plane had flown all day over Iraqi territory, and hadn't caught a whisker of flak. He gave the engine a pat, moving to the forked tail at the rear of the plane. He touched it gently, almost kneading the metal the way an experienced cowboy might massage a trusted but slightly tired horse. Then the pilot gave the right rudder a good hard slap and continued around the plane, making sure she was ready to go. He touched the pitot head gingerly, and practically saluted the AN/ALQ-119 ECM pod that hung off the right wing—Shotgun believed in wallowing in the mud, but there was nothing wrong with sending out a good swath of electronic interference while you are doing it, especially when the enemy was spitting flak and missiles at you.

Back at the nose of the plane, he gave the cannon a good tug, just to let it know he was counting on it. Satisfied that the Warthog was ready to go, Shotgun pulled on his helmet and gave his flight gear a quick check—the last thing he wanted was to misplace his Three Musketeers bar during combat. Satisfied that he was ready to go, the pilot hoisted himself up onto the wing and clambered atop the plane. He settled against the fuselage, legs extended out from the wing root, head back, trying to grab a Z or two while he waited for the colonel to arrive with the Mavericks.

Hope Goose is half as comfortable as this, he thought as his eyelids closed.

33

Sergeant Clyston took a turn around the back end of the avionics shop, making sure there were no problems before heading out to find Colonel Knowlington. He hadn't decided on what he was going to do or even say; probably the words wouldn't be near as important as the glance that would pass between them.

The Hog was a fantastically tough airplane, not only designed to withstand hot zones, but also made to be easily maintained during war. Still, she couldn't quite take care of herself, and people like Technical Sergeant Rosen were critical to keeping the squadron in the air.

Which was why he put up with her.

"Sergeant, we need more tacan fins," she complained as soon as she spotted him.

"Why? We lose one?"

"Not yet. But—"

"Don't be jinxing me with that kind of talk then," said Clyston, sliding away. He could see the colonel walking from the hangar where he'd suited up for the flight.

"Yah, Sergeant, I ha-fkt a problem with a wing hinch," said one of Clyston's chiefs, a geezer named Tinman who knew nearly as much about the planes as Clyston but was considerably better with an acetylene torch. Tinman's only drawback was his thick accent, which few could easily identify, much less decipher.

"Wing hinge? What the hell are you doing, making these planes ready for carrier duty?" Clyston asked.

"Daht Tomcat landed earlier. They askt me to inspect. I find dam-ach from flak."

"Okay, Tinman, I'll be with you in a second."

Clyston managed to squeeze away, and had Knowlington in sight when another of his sergeants, Pearlman Greene, tapped him on the shoulder. Greene's black face glistened with sweat and his eyes were narrowed down to slits.

"Sergeant, could I have a word?"

Greene wasn't the kind of guy who asked for "a word." Clyston realized immediately what was up—Greene headed the squadron's survival equipment shop and had undoubtedly rigged Mongoose's chute.

He let Greene lead him a few yards away, around the side of one of the hangars.

"You're supposed to be sleeping, Pearly," he said when the rigger finally stopped.

"I heard there wasn't a chute."

"Ah, shit, that's bullshit. Who told you that? Captain Wong? He's from the goddamn Pentagon. He doesn't know what's going on."

"Not Wong. Not an officer."

Clyston scowled, holding it a little longer in case Greene couldn't quite catch it in the darkness. "It's still bullshit. Was the guy there? No. Geez, you know how these rumors get going. How long you been in the Air Force?"

"I never lost a guy. Never."

"And you didn't now."

"I checked the rig as carefully as I could."

"I know you did, Pearly. Listen, if something fucked up, it wasn't the chute. I guarantee that. You're the best parachute rigger I ever met, and let me tell you, I've met a bunch. What the hell are you letting yourself worry for, huh? Crap, I guarantee the chute opened."

Greene didn't answer. A few guys, not many, but some, could totally divorce themselves from the job. Plane goes down, well, hey, that's show business.

Most, though, and certainly the ones the Capo di Capo wanted working for him, felt it to the core. Caring was part of what made them so good. Guys like that, you could logic them to death about how it wasn't their fault, and they still felt like they'd pulled the trigger on the SAM that took down the plane.

"Thing is, Shotgun saw the chute," offered Clyston.

"He did?"

"Damn straight. That's what I heard, and you know no one's lying to me and living to tell about it. Shotgun saw the ejection. Which means he saw the chute. You know Captain O'Rourke. He doesn't bullshit anybody, right?"

"Captain O'Rourke is okay."

"Damn straight he's okay. Listen, Johnson is on the ground cooking up some MREs right about now, probably heating them with one of your flares. Fucking officer, right?"

Greene laughed—weakly, but still it counted for something.

"Thing is, we're going to get him back," Clyston told him. "Colonel Knowlington's going up himself."

Even in the dark, Clyston could see Greene's face light up. "The colonel. Wow."

Clyston nodded solemnly. "You know if the colonel's going up there, Major Johnson is on the way back."

"No shit."

"So the chute must have worked. Because Knowlington isn't wasting his time heading into bad-guy land for someone who's not there."

"Yeah, no way. Not the colonel. And he'll get him back too."

"Damn straight. Go catch some Zs, Sergeant."

"I will. Thank you, Allen."

"Yeah, yeah," grunted Clyston, his legs already churning as he headed away.

•   •   •

By the time he found the colonel, Skull was partaking of a flight ritual his old crew chief recognized well from Thailand.

The preflight, below-wing pee. The good-luck piss. The best leak in the business, Knowlington called it.

Unofficially, of course. Doing your business on the edge of a runway wasn't something a pilot ever did under any circumstances ever, not in the jungle, not in the desert, not anywhere.

And luck? No officer of the U.S. military was that superstitious.

"Combat has some advantages, huh, Sergeant?" said Knowlington, his business done. His aw-shucks grin made him look twenty-three again. "Have to try that at Andrews sometime and see what the reaction is. What's up?"

"Nothin'."

"Plane looks like she's ready to fly. One of the candy men told me you have them rope on a pair of LUU-2 flares."

"Thought they might come in handy."

"I'm coming back," said the colonel, his tone changing abruptly. "Don't worry about me."

"I wasn't."

Knowlington laughed. "Sure you were. That was the first time in your life you took a compliment without growling. Make sure the rest of the planes get off okay. If the frag gets screwed up because I took the spares, someone's going to be pissed."

It wasn't like he'd come to say a lot, but Clyston found his tongue tied. "I will," he managed, smiling and stepping back. Two airmen came over to make some final check, and Clyston felt himself drifting back as the colonel jumped up the ladder and slipped inside the A-10A cockpit.

He really did seem like he was twenty-three again, full of vinegar. The old pros called him "Stick Boy."

Part of it was a compliment in honor of his flying skills. Part of it wasn't.

Long time ago, that. In those days, Clyston hadn't really thought of making the Air Force a career. But after Vietnam, it had just seemed to be the thing to do. No explaining why.

Preflight finished and plane ready to crank, Knowlington

gave them a thumbs-up as the Hog's rumble turned serious. The plane began edging toward the firing line, ready to launch itself into the darkness.

Chief Master Sergeant Allen Clyston stood and watched until the glow from the twin jets at the back of the plane vanished into specks smaller than the stars. Finally, he nodded, hitched up his pants, and turned to see about where in hell he could find a hinge for Tinman.

34

When it was obvious that the Scud alert was over, Lieutenant Dixon was the first to shed his gear. He'd had to scrunch over the entire time, and as fascinating as it was to hear a television correspondent explain what it was like to be scared shitless, Dixon couldn't help but think about the roast beef down the hall, getting cold.

According to CNN, Patriot missiles had nailed the incoming Scuds. There apparently hadn't been any chemicals in the warhead; at the moment, there didn't appear to be any casualties either. For all their value as propaganda weapons, the Scuds were fairly useless tactically, amounting to more of an annoyance than anything else.

Plus they pissed people off. Especially ones like Dixon who were waiting to eat roast beef for the first time in months.

Three British army officers were among the other guests, as were two very pretty women who had shown the poor taste of bringing their husbands along to eat with Fernandez, his wife, and their twelve-year-old son. The fact that the women were obviously spoken for made Dixon concentrate even harder on the meat.

Which turned out to be nice and hot and even juicier than his imagination had hoped. There were mashed potatoes and gravy, and even the carrots looked good. Steam wafted upwards from the dishes. Lush, sensual aromas filled the air, and for the first time in several days Dixon actually forgot about being stuck in Riyadh instead of flying a Hog.

Plate heaped high, the lieutenant barely managed to keep his hands together as one of the Fernandez neighbors launched into a brief benediction. He had just grabbed his fork when one of the two Pakistani servants appeared and announced that someone had come to the front door looking for Lieutenant Dixon of the U.S. Air Force.

"Me?" he pleaded, but the servant had not made a mistake. Dixon found an Air Force security captain and a pair of Army MPs standing in the front foyer.

"Lieutenant, I have orders for you."

"Now?"

"My understanding was this was to be expedited." The captain made an expression designed to convey the fact that he couldn't explain everything with Dixon's civilian host standing behind him. "That assignment you were waiting for?" he said. "Well, it's been approved."

"Darn." Dixon realized he was talking about the Special Ops gig. Talk about timing.

"Lieutenant?"

"It's just—I—roast beef."

"Yeah, smells good."

"We'll take up the slack for you, BJ," said Fernandez. "Open invitation. Come back anytime."

"How about a doggy bag?"

The captain hitched his fingers into his gun belt. "Say Lieutenant, no offense, okay, but I had to shanghai half the Army to come out and find you."

"All right, I'm sorry," said Dixon. "I'll follow you."

"No, sir. We'll have someone else take your vehicle back to Riyadh, if you don't mind."

Man, thought Dixon, attach the words "Special Ops" to something and people really got worried.

It would be different if he were going to go and get Mongoose. Undoubtedly the squadron DO had been picked up by now—or more likely, taken by the Iraqis. Even if he hadn't, it would take the better part of the night if not longer to drive all the way up to the advance base where the Pave Lows operated.

Probably, this was just part of Knowlington's backdoor plan to get him back to the base without raising any suspicions. But hell, couldn't it have waited until he finished dinner?

"Really, Captain, it's no sweat for me to take the car back to Riyadh myself," he said as he went out the front door.

"I doubt your vehicle will fit in the Huey," said the captain, pointing to the chopper revving on the front lawn.

35

In the dark, halfway up to KKMC, Skull felt one of the engines behind him stutter momentarily. It was an infinitesimal, practically unnoticeable thing, maybe an odd current that hit one engine only, or some microscopic impurity in the fuel. But it sent an icy shudder across his spine and around to his ribs; his chest and shoulder muscles spasmed and the darkness of the sky enveloped him. He became a rock, not a pilot. He could hear his breath in his ears and feel the mask pinch his face. His legs felt heavy, his arms paralyzed.

Until that moment, he hadn't worried about whether he could do this. He'd felt he had to, and that had been enough.

But now his muscles tightened, and he had to work to control his breathing. The plane was over whatever tiny stutter it had felt, but his was just beginning. He had to think about what he was doing—with his head as well as his hands and legs.

The Hog wasn't exactly a quick mover. Stable as hell, and predictable, but she cut through the blackness like a loaded dump truck working on three cylinders.

For a war zone, there were a hell of a lot of lights visible. And fires. Couple of good ones burning in Kuwait.

He'd poured the gas on to get away from the guns on the Laos ridge when his wingmate went down.

It wasn't that he was scared; it was that he'd been taken by surprise. His instincts took over.

And betrayed him.

Or showed who he truly was, beyond the bullshit and hype, beyond the luck. When you stood totally naked in front of the world, when it was all instinct, you couldn't lie to yourself.

There was a coward in him. He had to face that. They'd never recovered the crew and it was his fault.

Damn, he wanted a drink.

Fortunately, this was the one place in the world that he absolutely couldn't get one. Colonel Knowlington worked his eyes around the cockpit very deliberately, letting each needle and number soak into his brain before moving on. Everything was working at shop-manual specification; not bad for a plane that had received a new engine, new control surfaces, and sundry repairs within the past twenty-four hours.

If his math was correct, he had fifteen minutes to KKMC. Hog might actually be a bit faster than it seemed.

Two pilots had reported hearing fleeting transmissions over the emergency band as they returned from sorties up north. Whether they were Mongoose or not, no one could tell; they hadn't been much more than static, and they could even have been Iraqi. The fact that Mongoose's emergency beacon hadn't been picked up was not a good omen. Still, the news was vague enough to be interpreted either negatively or positively, and Skull chose positively.

His grip on the stick unclenched. He flexed his thumb back and forth, across, holding the plane's control stick firmly but gently. The thumb was one place he always got cramped in combat. As if all his tension went there.

You could live with that, though. He knew guys with back spasms. Now that was a ball-buster.

Bottom line was, he was bringing Mongoose home. His man, his responsibility. Some people might think he'd lost a step—he'd seen that question in Clyston's eyes—but they were wrong.

He did worry about his eyes. Vision was the reason he'd plunked MiGs two and three from the sky. The others, you could argue luck and flying skill, but two and three—he nailed them because he spotted them, saw the specks and knew instantly what their direction was, where their energy was pointed.

See the enemy first and he's yours; that was the old fighter-pilot maxim. And forget about 20-20 vision. You needed 20-10, at least.

Skull's were 20-05, X-ray sharp, on a bad day.

Maybe not now, though.

Didn't matter. Nothing really mattered, as long as he kept his muscles loose, worked the cockpit well, stayed within the limits of the plane.

He was going to get Mongoose back, or die trying.

Thing was, if he went out that way, then people really would think he was a hero.

A few might even be relieved.

Skull started to laugh.

Fourteen minutes to KKMC.

36

Mongoose clawed against the hard earth, pushing himself up the hill, away from the light, not even daring to pray that they hadn't seen him. Suddenly the ground disappeared and he felt himself falling forward, tumbling in confusion. Gunfire erupted behind the hill, but he barely heard it as he found his feet again and began to run.

What he did hear were the trucks. Their engines erupted as lights swung across the sky. The night turned reddish white—the Iraqis had fired a flare.

Open space lay in front of him. No trees, no rocks, no buildings, nowhere to hide.

His pistol was in his hand. He whirled, sighted toward the crest of the hill.

No one there.

Maybe they hadn't seen him after all. Maybe they weren't even here. Maybe this whole goddamn thing was a stinking mirage, the result of him hitting his head on the cockpit fairing or some such bullshit when he pulled the handle and got out of the plane.

Maybe he really wasn't in Iraq at all.

He started running again. The desert seemed to come up

around him, the flare starting to fade. He slipped on something, felt his ankle twist out from under him, had to put his hand out, and lost the pistol.

When he looked up, three men were standing in front of him, three rifles pointed directly at him less than ten yards away.

"You will surrender," said someone over a loudspeaker from the truck. The English was fairly good, with an American twist to the pronunciation. "You will give up now and you will not be harmed."

The Beretta was only a few inches from his fingers. He could reach it. He could get these guys.

"You will surrender now."

He glanced behind him, saw the other truck driving up. He rolled back on his butt, suddenly very tired.

When Mongoose didn't get up fast enough, one of the Iraqi soldiers pulled his rifle back to hit him. Another caught him, and an officer ran up and began berating the man, screaming something in his face. At the same time, a pair of arms took hold of Mongoose from the back, pulling him away and upward at the same time.

Something inside Mongoose snapped; he decided to try and shoot them all. He raised his arm and snapped his fingers closed, squeezing off the trigger.

Only to remember he had lost the gun.

The man pulling him backwards released him and he fell into a heap. Something heavy and hard caught him in the ribs. The blow pushed the air from his chest and he hunched toward his legs, gulping in pain, darkness edging the corner of his brain as if he were taking ten g's.

More yelling. Hands over him. Pulling and pushing. Somebody spat. He fought to breathe. His flight suit was searched with hard pats that were more like punches.

They were more than halfway done with their searching before his lungs started working again. By then he was on his back, an Iraqi on each arm and leg. He tried to get his head back into checklist mode, knew that was his job now. The anger had to be stowed where it couldn't hurt him.

When they released him, he rose slowly, standing with his arms held out in a gesture of surrender.

"You are our prisoner," said the man who had stopped the soldier from battering him. It was his voice he'd heard on the loudspeaker. His English was perfect, though he spoke very deliberately. "You will follow our orders precisely, or the consequences will be grave."

Mongoose said nothing, but did not offer any outward resistance. One of the trucks swung closer, illuminating the area with its headlights. Four or five Iraqi soldiers stood around him, well armed and equipped. Other men were continuing the search of the area.

"Where is your copilot?" asked the officer.

"I don't have a copilot," said Mongoose. "I fly alone."

"What type of plane do you fly?"

Mongoose hesitated. The truth was, his unit patch had a Warthog on it, so it wouldn't take much detective work to figure out the answer. But answering the question felt like surrendering.

"It's only got room for the pilot," he told the officer. "One man. Me."

"A fighter?"

"Yeah."

The officer nodded, and shouted something to the others. It might have been that he didn't trust Mongoose; their search continued.

The soldiers shifted, each staring openly at his face and uniform. One seemed angry; the rest looked merely curious, as if they were looking at a giant ape who had escaped from the zoo.

As long as the officer was here, Mongoose thought, he wouldn't be killed; he might not even be beaten. Most likely there was a reward for his safe return to Baghdad.

Or maybe not. Maybe the officer wanted to torture him himself.

When they had searched him, the soldiers had found and taken all of this important gear, including his radio, knife, and maps. But for some reason they'd missed his small flare gun, tucked into a leg pocket near his boot; he realized that as he stood uneasily in the semicircle of soldiers.

Something, at least.

They'd also taken Kathy's letter. But there wasn't much he could do about that.

One of the soldiers in the distance shouted. The officer motioned several of his guards toward the shouts, and they ran off. The search beam popped on and suddenly everyone was firing. Mongoose cringed, but tried otherwise not to react; he knew it was some sort of mistake, a false alarm. Instead, he focused his eyes on the ground, trying to think of something he could do.

No way he could run off and make it. He was pretty much stuck here.

It took the officer some minutes to calm his men. "You are not afraid?" he asked when he returned. His eyes were set wide in his face; up close he was a homely man, who didn't appear particularly wise or compassionate.

"I'm very afraid," Mongoose told him.

"You did not take cover when my men began to shoot?"

"Just now? I told you, there's no one else. They're shooting at shadows."

"A good thing for you," said the officer. He turned and shouted at the guards—apparently telling them to get up, since they did. He barked out more commands; all but two left to join the others.

The man seemed about Mongoose's age, maybe a little older. Barely five-eight, he was thin; his uniform hung around him as if meant for a heavier man.

"I could kill you," the officer told him.

"That's true," said Mongoose.

The officer smiled and nodded. "What is your name?"

"Major James Johnson."

"I am a major myself," said the man. He switched his pistol from his right hand to his left.

And then he extended his arm to shake Mongoose's hand.

Not knowing what else to do, Mongoose took it.

Had he thought about it, he might have expected something hard and callused. But this was soft and gentle, almost feminine.

The man smiled and nodded as he pulled back. Then he fished into his pocket and produced a blood chit—a note in

English and Arabic that promised a reward for his return to allied hands.

"What is this?" asked the Iraqi officer. It was obvious he had already read it; his voice sounded like a reprimand.

"My people will reward you for returning me safely."

The major made a show of ripping the note up and throwing it aside.

"And this?" He held up an envelope—Kathy's letter. "War plans?"

"A letter from my wife."

"You expect me to believe that?"

Mongoose shrugged. The man glanced at the letter, smiled, then held it toward him. Mongoose hesitated, then slowly took it.

After returning the envelope to his shoulder pocket, Mongoose looked up to see the Iraqi's pistol in his face.

"Do not think that because I show you kindness I am weak," said the man. "If you try to escape, you will be killed. You understand?"

He nodded.

"Into the truck."

With that, one of the other guards grabbed him roughly and pushed him toward the front of the open flatbed.

37

She saw them through the window. At first she thought the man and woman in the car were lost, looking for a neighbor's house. Then another car pulled up behind, followed by a van.

The van had a television station's logo on the side.

Robby stirred in her arms. He was hungry again. She sat on the couch, opened her blouse, and let him suckle. Ordinarily, he was more active in the afternoons, but he seemed to sense that his mother needed him to be calm. He poked her a few times with his hand, happy to be getting his milk, then settled back down.

Her in-laws were still out, not due back until five. The Air Force people, none of whom she knew, were on the way. The house was far from an air base, and because the squadron had been patched together at the last minute from other units and reserves, its stateside home base existed only on paper. Still, she knew the procession of blue cars would soon make their way through the twisty rural streets, hunting for the tiny house.

Part of her preferred to be alone, though now that the

reporters were outside she wasn't sure what to do. Sooner or later, one of them would ring the doorbell.

She'd locked the door earlier, but double-checked it now just to make sure.

When she realized that the commentators had no real news to report, Kathy had turned the sound off on the television. She kept glancing toward the screen every so often, however, alternately hoping for good news and dreading what she might see.

A new map of Iraq flashed on the screen, too vague to give any real idea of the country. It was followed by a picture of the A-10A lifted from Jane's, the encyclopedic military reference work. A retired Air Force colonel appeared on the screen, a man she hadn't seen in any of the sequences before.

The words, "Former POW," flashed under him.

Had Jimmy been captured? Was he alive?

She reached for the remote control, put the sound back on.

The phone rang as she did. She jumped up and startled the baby. He started to cry.

It was more a moan, forlorn and passive. Not his usual cry.

By the time she soothed him, the answering machine had picked up. A woman's voice came over the speaker. "Mrs. Johnson, my name is Teresa Fisher. I'm a reporter for WFDC over in Calhoon. We're very sorry to hear about your husband."

There were about a dozen reporters outside, the woman told the tape. They wouldn't come in and bother her, but if she wanted to say anything, they would be waiting outside. Three times the woman said she was sorry about her husband. Her voice sounded sincere.

"If you need anything," added the reporter, "let us know. We're sorry we're disturbing you. You should know that the whole country supports you. We've already had calls at the station, saying how much everyone is praying for you."

Kathy stared toward the kitchen hallway as the phone clicked off. Behind her on the TV, the newscaster was repeating that there was no new information about Major Johnson or the other pilots lost over Iraq.

Then he asked the retired Air Force officer about the possibility of torture.

Kathy pushed the red button on the remote, killing the power.

PART THREE

SMOKE 'EM
IF YOU SEE 'EM

38

Colonel Knowlington's eyes scratched at the sides of their sockets, straining in the darkness as they swept the cockpit instruments. His shoulder muscles were still a little tight, but otherwise he felt settled in the plane, the Warthog strapped around him. He couldn't quite tell the performance by feel alone yet—part of his problem was that he expected things to happen faster than they did—but maybe that was just as well; it meant he took less for granted.

Shotgun was in a combat trail not quite a mile behind him in the dark sky. They flew on silently, observing the general rule that unnecessary transmissions were almost always the ones the enemy used to home in on you.

One thing about the Gulf War that made it a hell of a lot different than Nam—Big Brother was definitely looking over your shoulder. There was an airborne controller working close in, and a fleet of AWACS charting everything but the pigeons from here to Berlin.

Pigeons probably had their own radar planes. Knowlington had always approved of the concept in theory—it greatly increased the odds of holding off enemy interceptors, which in turn meant better survivability. But it also chipped away at a pilot's autonomy. Skull had been taught that individual initiative was the cornerstone of successful air combat—in contrast to the heavily orchestrated and ground-controlled Soviet system. The fact that information from the AWACS on station was relayed back to the command center in Riyadh meant that it could easily be fed to Washington, D.C. Given what had happened in Vietnam, the colonel shuddered at the possibility of some White House janitor helping coordinate the air war on a rainy Sunday afternoon.

That hadn't happened yet, at least. The two Hogs of Devil flight had full autonomy to carry out their mission as an unscripted part of the search-and-rescue team.

Knowlington wanted a drink, but he could deal with that. It was like dealing with the SA-2's or -8's or -13's or Rolands, except that the launch warning was always sounding. You did your jinks, threw your chaff, lit your flares—

Nix the flares at night. Blind the shit out of you. And useless against a radar missile.

Skull rechecked his position on the INS, making sure he was precisely on beam. They were at eighteen thousand feet, which in his mind felt low, though it was near the top of the Hog's comfortable operating envelope. Fires burned in small sparkles in the distance; bulky shadows stretched out around them. Knowlington resisted the impulse to assign positions to the shadows; it was too easy to get the wrong idea stuck in your head. Better to stick to the abstract numbers.

His pulse hadn't picked up yet. He figured it would eventually. The adrenaline would start pushing into his stomach. There'd be a quick shock of fear, a motivator, not a paralyzer.

He could deal with fear. He'd been afraid before, plenty of times. Being afraid was familiar.

You took that whale breath, blew it out, let the muscle spasms pass through your system. You went through the wall and on the other side there was perfect clarity.

Usually.

Way point reached. Skull pushed the Hog gently, easing her left wing toward the earth as he brought her onto the prearranged course for the crash site. The plane slipped into the long, shallow glide as smoothly as a canoe edging onto a quiet lake.

The A-10A had two personalities. One was balls-out mud-fighting bitching, in Saddam's face screaming. The other, a surprise to Knowlington, was actually gentle. Partly it was her responsiveness to the controls, her tendency to go where you told her. Partly too, it might have been her lack of top-end. But there was something else there, as if the plane were as human as he was. Maybe it too was trying to monitor the emergency frequency, listening for the piercing squeak of the rescue beacon or, better, Mongoose's familiar voice.

Nothing but static. Knowlington worked his controls carefully, putting his eyes around the cockpit and going through his paces, getting ready for the adrenaline. This was a marathon race, and they hadn't even gotten to the start line yet.

There were sparkles far, far off in the distance. Somebody was taking flak.

Or more likely, an Iraqi gunner was spooked.

If the Hog's navigational systems were working properly, they were now about two miles from the spot Mongoose and Shotgun had been attacking when the plane went down. The colonel eased the Hog's throttle off further; they were making 305 knots and crossing seven thousand feet. The planes could not be heard above five thousand, and in the dark with their blackish green camo they were essentially invisible to anyone without radar. They'd trace out the attack route as closely as possible at this altitude, then gradually bring it down.

Skull definitely wanted to bring it down; while they were still in bad-guy country and ought not push their luck too far, he figured the Hogs' rumble would be instantly recognizable to Mongoose. If anything would provoke a flare, the hum of two Hogs would.

The seeker head in the Maverick found the wrecked overpass still hot from its pounding late yesterday; it was a fuzzy collection of wrecked debris in the small television monitor on the right side of the dash. Knowlington kept it on what passed for wide magnification, easing the Hog toward it with the fascination of a diver approaching an ancient wreck.

"How are we looking?" asked Shotgun over the squadron's common frequency as they pushed over the wreckage of the overpass.

"I have the dummy missiles or what's left of them," said Skull. "Bunch of roadway. Maybe the two carriers, I think. A couple of trucks. There's the Roland launcher. Broke it in half. Good shooting."

"Wish I'd gotten it sooner."

"You hear anything on Guard?" Skull asked.

"Nah. You?"

"No. Keep listening."

"You too."

"I'm turning," said Knowlington, moving to follow the path they believed Mongoose had taken when he was hit. He felt the prick of adrenaline in his stomach as the Maverick screen traced the ground into blankness.

39

Shotgun wanted a flare. A little Mark 79 pencil flare, shooting up to six hundred feet, sparkling for four or five seconds before dying out. A big Mark 13 would be even better. Those suckers lasted forever and you could see them from Washington, D.C.

Hell, he'd even settle for a strobe.

But the darkness gave him nothing back. The pilot gripped his stick tighter, following the colonel around the shoot-down area about three quarters of a mile for another circuit. Scanning the ground with the TVM was slow work, a bit like panning for gold.

A shitload of guys had already been over this, but they weren't Hog drivers. Not that they lacked motivation or expertise or anything like that; they just weren't part of the Hog brotherhood. Brothers felt stuff other relatives didn't, simple as that. If he hadn't been able to find him before, that was just because Mongoose was busy, maybe evading the enemy or something.

So give me a stinking flare, Goose Boy.

"Let's get low enough for him to hear us," said the

colonel, who started tilting the Hog's nose downward as he spoke.

"Exactly what I was thinking," said Shotgun. He glanced at the radio controls, gave it more volume. The emergency band stayed silent: no chirp, no voice, no nothing.

Hot damn, Goose. Get your butt out of that pup tent and flag us down. My Big Mac's getting cold, bro.

He ran his eyes around the ground. He'd have preferred having one of the Mavericks himself. Knowlington had told him switching them around would have cost them too much time, and even laughed when Shotgun told him he could set it up himself.

Which he could have, no sweat.

Shotgun willed his eyes into full-blown owl mode as he stared from the cockpit. Maybe from now on he'd carry some carrots with him, get that extra night-light boost.

Hell, if only he had found an Apache pilot and made that trade. It was top priority when he got back.

Better yet, go mail order and buy himself a pair of starlight goggles. There'd be complications with the instrument glow, but hell, Clyston or one of his guys could figure that out.

Maybe they could take whatever the gizmo was that worked the damn thing and expand it to fit the glass of the canopy. So you could have an entire panel of night vision.

That was what he was talking about.

Give me a flare, Mongoose. One lousy, stinking flare. That's all I'm sayin'.

40

By the time the Huey landed, Dixon had realized he wasn't being clandestinely ferried back to the home drome, machinations or not. They had flown northwest, and at top speed; by his calculations Iraq was about half a stone's throw away. He decided that clearance for the Special Ops Scud mission must have come through; his reward—or maybe punishment—was to be granted observer status on the first mission.

Not that he was objecting, but . . .

The Huey hulked in close to the dark hulk of a fat MH-53J. Originally drawn up as a heavy-lifter, the long-distance helicopter was bigger than a diesel locomotive and a couple of times more powerful. Something like fifty-five troops could crowd into the back, along with the three-man crew. Her real asset, however, was the powerful, long-range electronics and sensors that provided the "Pave Low" designation.

He wasn't sure it was the right helicopter or even if he really, truly, should be here. But since he didn't see any other helicopters nearby, Dixon jumped out and ran for it.

He kept his head down though there was plenty of clearance.

"Hey, you Dixon?" said the sergeant at the door.

"Yeah?"

"Well, come on, Lieutenant. We've been waiting for you."

The sergeant grabbed hold of his arm and yanked him not only into the Pave Low, but practically through to the other side. At the last second, he managed to change his momentum, and found himself stumbling toward the front of the big warbird. Just as he was about to steady himself on a bar near the cockpit, the big bird lifted off. Dixon bounced to his left, then flew back to the right as the helo's massive rotors beat the air. He slipped and rolled onto something hard.

It turned out to be the floor.

"What the hell you doin' down there, BJ?" asked the pilot—his old root-beer-drinking buddy Major Greer.

"I heard the floors on these things were clean enough to eat off," grunted Dixon, trying to get to his feet despite a fresh jink.

Dixon, who had been aboard a Super Jolly Green Giant before, knew that the choppers could fly relatively smoothly, even when they were moving fast. Apparently Greer hadn't read that part of the sales brochure.

"About time you got up here," said Greer. "I been waiting half the night for you."

"Scud attack hung me up."

"See? I told you. If we were going for them, you wouldn't have to put up with that bullshit anymore."

"We're not going after the Scuds?"

"Hell, no. At least, not tonight. We're going to go fetch us a Hog driver. Nobody told you?"

"Mongoose?"

"That Major Johnson?"

"Yup."

"That's who we're getting."

"You found him?"

"I didn't say we found him. I said we were going to go get

him. I've been waiting for word that he was found. Lucky
for you it didn't come or we would have been gone."

Dixon wondered to himself if the other half of that
equation meant Mongoose had been unlucky.

"We'd like to make the pickup in the dark," added the
helicopter pilot. "Less people to shoot at us. Sun won't
come up until almost oh-five-thirty. But we'll have some
fog after that, most likely, so we have some leeway."

"Has he been spotted yet?"

"No. But we want to get closer so we can make a quick
pickup. Saddam won't mind if we hang out over the fence,
you think?"

"Nah."

"Word is your colonel knows where he is. Went to mark
the way for us."

"Colonel Knowlington? No shit."

"If we get lucky, we may smoke a stinking Scud launcher
on the way back," said the major. "Then we'll all be heroes.
Sergeant, fix him up, would you? And keep him calm.
Dixon here blasted an Iraqi Hind the other day and word is
he's bucking for the Medal of Honor. I don't want him
falling out of my aircraft until we're back home."

41

The trucks were old military-model flatbeds—Soviet, he thought, or maybe French—though as far as Mongoose was concerned, their most notable feature was the particularly uncomfortable ribbed metal bed in the back. He sat against the wall of the cab, opposite his two guards, who were crouched a short distance away. Five or six other soldiers clung to various parts of the open back. They didn't have to grip too hard; the truck was moving at a snail's pace, following in the dark behind the vehicle equipped with the searchlight. Neither truck seemed to have a muffler, and both were running rougher than the old Camaro Mongoose had owned in high school. Maybe the four hours they'd spent sitting idle as the Iraqis searched for his nonexistent copilot had fouled their plugs.

When they had captured him, Mongoose had assumed the men were part of the Iraqi Republican Guard, crack troops equipped with the best weapons and generally regarded as the best disciplined soldiers in the army. Now he wasn't so sure. He'd seen pictures of the Guards where they were wearing berets; there were no berets in sight, and in fact most of these men had fairly plain uniforms. Most seemed barely teenagers, not the hardened veterans who had fought the Iranians to a standstill.

His guards had rolled the cuffs of their khaki pants away from the heels of their boots. Even in the dim light, he could tell the ends were frayed. One of the men made an effort to frown every time he caught Mongoose looking at him. The other just stared.

The soldier who had tried to hit him was in the other vehicle. The men on this truck were more curious than angry, and if it weren't for the roar of the poorly tuned truck motor, he might have tried striking up a conversation. Mongoose figured their curiosity was more or less in his favor; it might make them less inclined, or at least less quick, to shoot him.

There had been no interrogation yet. The officer hadn't seemed much interested in doing anything but making sure he was alone, and then taking him back to wherever they were going in one piece.

But the questioning would surely come. And it wouldn't necessarily be pleasant.

Mongoose knew a great deal about the Hogs, their tactics, and the general situation, but he hardly possessed any great military secrets. Even so, he wanted to give up as little as possible. He certainly wouldn't volunteer information. But he had to be realistic; it would be impossible to say absolutely nothing if the Iraqis began torturing him. It was a question of how long he could hold out, and what information he could hold back.

Part of him wanted to jump up and dive over the side of the truck right now, make a desperate, foolhardy attempt to escape. But his job wasn't to do something stupid; it was to survive.

Kath needed him to survive. So did Robby.

Every night before turning in, Mongoose sat in his tent and wrote a just-in-case letter, a last word to his wife in case he didn't make it back. Knowlington would probably have it by now.

Knowlington. His opinion of the commander had changed somewhat since the fighting started. The colonel actually had done a decent job pulling the unit together; only two months ago it had been organized only on paper, a discordant melange of planes destined for the junk heap with barely enough men to get them there. As Knowlington's second-in-command, Johnson had done a lot of the work in Saudi Arabia himself, especially with the pilots, but he had to admit ol' Skull had a good way about him. He knew just about everybody in the Air Force, and between him and Sergeant Clyston—a man whose rating seemed to stretch into triple digits—the unit was the best supplied on the base, maybe in the entire Air Force. Plus Knowlington just about glowed reassurance, spreading calm and patience wherever he went. Despite all his personal problems, the guy had seen this shit before; he put it in perspective. He thought before he spoke, and actually listened to what people told him.

Maybe too much, since he had been known to ask an airman what he thought, and actually consider the advice. The colonel wasn't by-the-book enough for Mongoose's taste, not by a mile. And then there was the drinking, which wasn't much of a secret, though he seemed to have knocked it off since coming to the war zone.

But Knowlington's biggest knock was the fact that he was a low-timer in the Hog; some of the mechanics probably had flown more. He was an outsider, a fast-mover pilot and commander who'd ended up heading the A-10 squadron—technically, it was a wing, though only at squadron force—completely by accident. If it hadn't been for a last minute request by Schwarzkopf himself, Knowlington would have overseen these planes' flight to the boneyard, not Iraq. Whoever had cut the original orders had basically intended him to be a junkyard foreman, not a combat commander.

But he was a combat commander, and not a bad one. Maybe a real good one. He'd gone through hell in Vietnam, with medals and scars to prove it. He was a real pilot, probably a hero once.

Shit, someday they might say that about Mongoose.

Assuming he made it back.

Checklist. Stay in the here and now.

Mongoose caught an image of himself with a sign around

his neck that said he was a war criminal. For some reason he also saw himself naked—and began to laugh.

The guards looked at him as if he was laughing at them. But he couldn't stop himself. It seemed like the most hilarious thing in the world, him naked.

Ten or fifteen minutes later, Mongoose was jerked against the cab as the truck stopped short with a crash, rear-ending the one it had been following. The pain in his head, which had subsided almost to the point where he didn't notice it, returned with a vengeance. His knee gave a fresh twinge of pain.

Both of his guards fell at his feet. They weren't curious now—they grabbed him viciously and pulled him from the flatbed.

"I didn't do it," he said, holding out his hands. "Please. My leg."

In the next moment he was tossed over the side. He couldn't get his arms out in front of him quickly enough, and the bottom of his jaw snapped upwards, barely missing his tongue, but hurting like all hell anyway. Arms grabbed him and hauled him to his feet; finally a shout from the captain made his captors ease up.

The truck ahead had blown a tire. He thought for a moment that they were going to put him to work changing it, but the soldiers did that themselves after pulling the two vehicles apart. The officer in charge passed by him, shaking his head.

He returned a few minutes later and asked if Mongoose wanted a cigarette.

"Don't smoke," said Mongoose.

"Bad for your health, right?" The man took a pack of Marlboros from his pocket and carefully removed a cigarette. "Very difficult to get these days," he told Mongoose. "American-dog cigarettes. But we all need our luxuries."

"How do you know English?"

"Everyone knows English." As he lit the cigarette, the man's face glowed red. It was not a gentle face, despite his manner. "I went to college at Iowa State. I am an engineer."

"And you came back?"

"Wouldn't you?"

No, he wouldn't, thought Mongoose, and then he realized that of course he would—he would return to his home and family.

"A materials engineer. I could be in great demand in Europe. But there are always complications," said the officer. "Yourself?"

"I'm just a pilot."

"Where did you go to school?"

Mongoose hesitated, considering whether the information might somehow help his captor. Probably not, only in the vague way of helping to build rapport. But that probably cut both ways; it might make the man more trusting, and easier to lie to.

"RPI," he told him. "I was an engineering major too."

"Really? Very good. Very good." The officer nodded, then took a long drag from his cigarette. It seemed as if he was going to say more, but one of his men called him over to the truck.

They'd taken Mongoose's watch with everything else, so he wasn't sure what time it was. From the sky, he guessed that it might be an hour before dawn, somewhere in the long twilight before the sun rose.

If these guys were Muslims—and that seemed a damn good bet—they'd stop for morning prayers. Might be a good time to try running for it.

Why not try now then? The ground sloped off from the road. The shadows thickened a short distance away.

The running lights of the nearby truck flashed on as the motor came to life.

He caught some low-slung shadows ahead in the strands of moonlit night fog. Buildings, maybe a city or a unit headquarters of some type.

His destination?

The truck at the front coughed a few times, but refused to start. The motor wound into an incessant whine.

The sound reminded him of a moment two years before, the winter, his wife having trouble and flooding the car.

He pushed the idea away. Here and now. Checklist mode. The officer shouted to his men as the battery's charge ground down. A group went to the back of the truck, as if they were going to push it, and then jump-start it.

That'll never work, Mongoose thought to himself. But then the AAA probably didn't offer roadside assistance out here.

As he watched them grunt and groan the vehicle forward, he heard a low, almost guttural hum in the distance.

A Hog.

Was he dreaming it? He looked toward the sky.

The truck engine sputtered and coughed, then somehow caught. He strained to hear over the sound. For undoubtedly the first time in his life he cursed the fact that the A-10A's turbofans were relatively quiet.

The truck drowned out whatever he had heard. If he had heard anything.

Run for it?

One of his guards put his rifle into Mongoose's side and prodded him toward their vehicle. He kept his eyes trained toward the sky for another second, desperate to see something.

The guard pushed him forward.

"Into the truck, let's go," the Iraqi major told him. "Now, Major."

"I have to take a leak," said Mongoose, desperate to hear the noise again.

"You can relieve yourself when we arrive at our headquarters. It won't be long."

"But—"

"I should not like to shoot you, but I will certainly do so if you do not get on the truck." The Iraqi had his hand on his pistol.

Mongoose held his hands out. "I'm sorry," he said, turning and repeating the words to his guards. Then he pulled himself up onto the truck, hesitating for just a second as he got his legs under him, wincing because of his knee, and willing the Hog to return.

42

Skull leaned into the Maverick's screen, trying to sort out the shadow. It was small and faint, but wouldn't that be what a body would look like? It was about a mile east of a trio of abandoned, probably burnt-out buildings. That was exactly where a pilot hoping to vector a rescue helicopter in might end up—close enough to give the helicopters an easy landmark, but not too close to be found when the enemy searched the obvious hiding places.

Colonel Knowlington pitched the plane around and had it move through the bank quicker than he expected; he fought the impulse to snap back, let himself ease onto the new course. He was right about the similarities with the old Spad. Not that you flew it the same, of course; it was more the way you thought about it, more the mind-set. You saved those hard turns for when you were walking through shit.

"We got something?" Shotgun asked.

"Not sure. Something warm, but I can't tell yet. East of the buildings."

"This is still a little south of where he'd be," said Shotgun. "But he could have walked down. Makes sense."

Skull was too busy trying to wish the shadowy fuzz into

focus to answer. The seeker head in the Maverick had been designed to home in on hot tank engines, and in fact all the experts said it could absolutely not be used as a night-vision device. As much as Knowlington would love to prove them wrong, he had to admit they had a point.

"Hey, we got something moving on the road ten, maybe twelve miles south," said Shotgun. "Uh, nine, ten o'clock."

Skull immediately changed course. This time, there was no question what he was looking at—though it still felt a little like staring at an X-ray machine on monochrome acid.

"Yeah, okay," he told Shotgun. "Two trucks. Not very fast." He glanced back at the artificial horizon, made sure he was level—without real points of reference and your eyes on the TV screen, it was very easy to get discombobulated. But his sense of balance was still at spec—his wings were perfectly paralleling the ground.

"They must be coming for him," said Shotgun.

The IR seeker glowed with the two vehicles moving slowly along the highway. The Hogs were approaching from seven o'clock at about eight thousand feet, moving at 320 knots. Knowlington flicked the viewer into narrow mode, increasing the magnification to six times but temporarily losing the trucks because the view was narrower. He held his course and they reappeared, fat and slow.

They might be going for Mongoose, but only if that shadow was really him. They might also just be passing through. They were still pretty far off; odds were they'd miss him, even if they searched the buildings.

Attack them and anyone in range of their radio might put things together.

Or not. Best just to splash them. Odds were they were working alone.

"We'll do a quick circuit, see what else is around," Skull told him. "You hear the beacon yet?"

"Negative. I keep trying."

"Me too."

They passed over the two trucks and rode out about eight miles before banking back. There didn't seen to be anything else out here.

Plinking the truck with the Maverick was child's play.

You flagged the crosshairs onto the target and locked it; the missile took care of the rest. Skull pushed the nose of his Hog down, accelerating slightly as he came back around toward the truck from the northeast. He had 5,500 feet, no wind to speak of, a nice smooth ride, and a good view of the trucks on the screen. He was lower than he probably had to be, but that would only increase his accuracy.

Skull locked on the engine, ready to fire.

As he closed he reconsidered the situation. There were only two Mavericks aboard. He had to keep one if he was going to use it to see. That meant he had only one shot, and it seemed like a waste to take out such a soft target with it.

Better to use the cannon. Except that it was dark and they'd have to go even lower.

"Whatchya doin', Skip?" asked Shotgun.

"I don't think these guys are worth a missile," said Skull.

"They're heading toward Goose. I can feel it," said Shotgun.

Skull pulled the Hog's nose up, breaking his approach and swinging back to the north. "Want to get some shooting in?" Knowlington asked his wingman.

"Shit, yeah."

"Here's the game plan. We'll go back, fly a trail, you behind me. Get good separation. I'll hit a flare; you come in and smoke 'em. If we time it right, you should be able to splash both trucks on one pass. I'm pulling up and to the left; you go right."

"I'm with you, Colonel. Let's do it."

"Watch your eyes. If you're blinded, pull off and take another turn. I'll be spinning around for your six."

"Sounds good."

Skull brought his Hog onto the course and reached for the throttle, pulling it out and bringing the nose down at the same time. The plane jumped downward, air shrieking around her as she bolted into the attack. He used the Maverick screen to help measure the distance, one finger up on the panel to kick out the LUU-2 flare. The Hog was low enough to be heard, and he expected ground fire at any second. It wouldn't amount to anything but an annoyance—

unless, of course, one of the Iraqis was packing the silver bullet.

Silver bullet came and got you no matter what. So you couldn't waste your worry on that one.

Knowlington focused on the screen. He pushed himself down into the seat, trying to melt himself into the plane, make his muscles merge with it. The trucks glowed brighter and brighter in the TVM. He was just about to pass them and he yanked the stick—too hard, he could tell—but he caught it quick, fired the flare, and now had his hands full, the Hog bucking above the flash, and temporarily he was lost and there was light everywhere and something popped in his head, a light snap and a burst, a thin string breaking and he was in control, flying the plane, pushing up through five and then six thousand feet, going faster than he expected and banking into a turn, positioning himself to watch Shotgun's butt but also to step in if he missed.

43

This time, he knew it was a Hog, and he knew it was coming back. It came at him close and sudden, and he jumped to his feet in the moving truck, as excited as if a guardian angel had suddenly appeared in the sky. He pitched around toward the front of the truck, looked over the cab into the darkness, up at the crescent moon. He thought he saw the plane's shadow pass in front, the moon winking at it as it dove to rescue him, thought he felt the thick wings of the Hog swoop to grab him and pluck him to safety.

In the next second, an LUU-2 parachute flare exploded overhead, the light of two million candles turning the desert brighter than a ballpark during the World Series. His whole face stung with the sudden light. Rifles next to him started to fire.

Then he realized what was happening:

The Hogs were going to smoke the truck.

Head down, still temporarily blinded, he pushed to get away, leaping and flailing toward the side of the vehicle. The earth roared behind him, hell opening up and spitting sulfur. Major James "Mongoose" Johnson felt himself lifted up. He flew through the air, brimstone and molten metal stinging his nostrils.

44

When she'd told them she'd speak at nine p.m., it had seemed like a very long time off. But it was here, and even though she had nothing to say, nothing more than she could have said a few hours ago, Kathy Johnson felt as if she had to keep her commitment. She pushed the palms of her hands across her freshly laundered blue skirt and stood up from the couch.

Jean, her mother-in-law, turned her face from the television screen and looked up from her side.

"It's time," Kathy told her.

None of the others moved, not her father-in-law Bob, on the small upholstered chair, or the two Air Force officers on the love seat at the far end of the room. Major Barbara Figundo, an information specialist and PR troubleshooter, stood in the door frame to the kitchen, where she had been helping herself to a sandwich.

"I'm ready," Kathy said.

"You don't have to go out there if you don't want to," said Figundo.

"I told them I would."

"It's still your call. You're in charge."

Kathy had no idea who might really be in charge of this thing, but it wasn't her. "How's my makeup?"

"Perfect," said Jean.

"Looks good," said the major.

Kathy walked toward the door, pausing to catch her reflection in the mirror that hung near the far hallway.

She was still heavy from the baby. The knit sweater, a light blue, hid a bit of her midsection. Her hair needed to be cut, but she looked presentable.

The newspeople on the front lawn let out a shushing noise as she came out from the house, a cross between a sigh and a deep breath. They stood back a moment as she stepped forward, as if they were surprised she had remembered she'd said she would come out. Kathy gave a kind of half wave to the policeman, and then beckoned the media people forward as if she were signaling to a shy child.

No shy child would have moved so quickly up the lawn. By now there were more than two dozen reporters from all media, as well as their assorted camera crews and assistants. They came right up to the steps, barely leaving her six inches worth of personal space as they jostled to get their microphones and cameras into position. She smiled as best she could, waiting for them to settle in. When one or two pushed forward a little too close, she held her hand out, motioning them around like Halloween trick-or-treaters who'd gotten a little too eager for their candy.

She waited until everyone stopped fussing. It was remarkable what good manners they actually had.

She saw her breath in front of her as she opened her mouth to speak.

"My name is Kathleen Johnson and obviously you know why I'm here," she heard herself say.

It was a good start. She remembered tricks from her college speech class—look people in the eye, be upbeat, replace the ums and uhs with pauses—silence looked smart.

"I really can't say anything beyond what the Air Force has told you. My husband was a pilot when I met him and I've understood the risks since before we were married. He has an important job to do and . . . the, uh, the other members of the squadron are professionals and they have a job to do too."

Her voice wavered. All of a sudden she wasn't sure what she was talking about—professionals? Well, of course they were, but what was the point?

She could feel her lips starting to waver.

She was out here not just to answer questions, but to inspire others who might be in the same position. She couldn't break down; that wouldn't inspire anyone, except maybe the people who shot down her husband.

She wanted to call an end to this quickly, but stopping would just make it worse. She ducked her head ever so slightly the way a horse might during a tough part of a race. "I'm sure Jimmy will be back in one piece very, very soon," she said. "In the meantime, I'm fine and the rest of the family is fine. We appreciate the country's concern."

She smiled. Good enough.

She reached behind her for the door handle.

"You have no information on where your husband went down?" asked a reporter.

It caught her slightly off guard. "Of course not," she said. "And if I did, do you really think I would broadcast it to Saddam? He's sure to be watching these reports. The man is a murderer; I'm not going to lead him to my husband."

"The Air Force won't tell you?"

The major bristled beside her; Kathy squeezed her arm before she could say anything. "The Air Force has been exceedingly helpful. They're family," she said, her voice sharp. "Are there other questions?"

"How is your little boy?" asked a woman reporter on her left. She recognized the voice—it was the person who had left the phone message.

"Well, almost sleeping through the night these days," Kathy told her.

It was the same thing she told all the relatives—but the reporters took it as a joke and laughed.

"I remember those days," said the woman.

"Could we have his age?" asked a man near her.

"Three months. Almost four."

"Wow. That's tough."

"A lot of military families have more children and are in the same position as I am—well, almost the same," Kathy said. "What about you? Do you have children?"

"Two. And the first one had colic. I don't think my wife or I slept for the first six months."

"He took after his dad," quipped one of the other reporters. The others laughed.

"Well, Robby doesn't have colic, thank God," said Kathy. "But I really should get back to him. Are there other questions?"

"Has the President called yet?" said a man on her right.

"Why would the President call?" she asked him. His face looked vaguely familiar; Kathy believed she had seen him on TV, but couldn't quite place him.

"He said he would."

"Could we listen in?" asked the jerk who had wanted her to direct Saddam to her husband.

"I'm sure anything he'd have to say would be private," said Kathy. "And anything I'd say would be trivial. I don't think he's calling; I mean, I wouldn't think he would. Not for this. It's not—it's not necessary."

She felt her lip quivering. The Air Force people hadn't told her about the President.

She didn't think he'd be calling if it was good news.

The moon, a flat yellow crescent, caught her eye. Its glow seemed to brighten for a moment, twinkling with an obscure reflection. It warmed her, helped her catch her lip. She stared at it for a moment, wondered at how far away it was, how it hung there, constant.

"All right," she said, feeling exactly how heavy and cold her hands had become. She wrapped them together across her chest. "I'm going back now. Thank you for coming."

Thank you for coming? But what else would you say? She gave one last smile, then turned to the door.

"When will you talk to us again?" asked the jerk.

Never to you, she thought. But the cameras were still rolling; she didn't want it to look as if she were running away.

"In the morning, unless I need you to watch the baby," she said.

"Hey, I'm good at burping kids," said the reporter whose child had been colicky. "Let me know if you need help."

The others laughed and she smiled, squeezing back through the door.

Kathy took two steps inside before she began to shake. A moment later, she found herself crying on her father-in-law's shoulder, nearly out of control even as he told her she had done real fine.

45

The first truck frothed beneath the weight of the bullets, crackling into dust as Shotgun stood on the rudder pedals, walking the cannon back and forth through the son of a bitch like working a drill into a piece of diseased wood. His eyes stung a bit from the flare, and the world had a washed-out tint to it, but he wasn't pausing even to blink them now, keeping the A-10 in her dive as he eased off the trigger, giving the gun a brief rest before picking up the second truck. The bullets skipped out of the plane again, the kick pushing the Hog back as if the force of the gun alone could keep the plane in the air.

Shotgun started to drift off target, and realized he was running out of space; he held on for just a half second more, squeezing off a good burst before yanking into his escape. He pushed the plane for all she was worth, vulnerable now; he'd wiped the trucks but there was always a chance, remote but there, that some patriotic Iraqi had scrounged an SA-16 and managed to survive the onrush of uranium and high-explosives. The plane's nose sniffed for the darkness; she welcomed the cover like a real warthog escaping into the bushes.

Somebody was aiming at him. He felt a flash from behind, small for a rocket and well behind him, but coming for him nonetheless. Without hesitating or waiting for Skull's warning, he goosed off some decoy flares and gave the Hog all the throttle she would take. Shotgun closed his eyes against the new flare's light, but even when he opened them the glare was worse than flying through a blizzard with a pair of arc lamps strapped to the fuselage. It took an eternity for the plane to get away. His eyes struggled to regain their night vision; he couldn't even see his instruments.

Not that he needed them. This morning the Hog was just about flying herself. She did that when the stakes got high enough. The plane wagged her fanny in the air as she climbed, now out of range of any shoulder-fired heat-seeker. From her point of view, it hadn't taken long to get away at all. From her point of view, her pilot said go and she went.

As Shotgun brought the plane around and began looking for his lead, he saw that one of the two trucks had caught fire.

He decided he'd get the other on his next swing.

"What was with the flares?" asked Skull

"I felt something."

"I had your six. Bring your course around another forty degrees."

"I was thinking another pass."

"Negative," snapped the colonel. "You wiped their asses on your first pass. No sense wasting any more bullets. You see me yet, or you need me to key the mike?" he added, offering to use the radio as a crude direction-finder, since the A-10A's gear could show the direction of transmission.

"No, I got you," said Shotgun.

"We're going over that spot near the buildings with a fine-tooth comb."

"Listen, I didn't mean that I thought you wouldn't warn me if someone was shooting at me. I just had a hunch, like I felt something coming off the ground for me."

Knowlington didn't bother answering.

46

Mongoose landed arm-first, felt a bone in the forearm snap.

His head blanked. His whole body moved away from him. Dirt pushed into his nose and mouth. He bit the inside of his lip, felt the dizziness come, rolled.

The pilot remembered the flares tucked inside his flight suit. He got to his knees and reached for the bandolier. Halfway there the pain overwhelmed him and his right arm fell limp; he fell forward onto his head, scraping against the dirt. Bent into the earth, resting on his shoulder, he reached for the flares with his good hand, tearing at his suit to retrieve them.

There was shouting and moaning and crying behind him. The A-10's had pulled off, probably to line up for another pass. They'd see the flare if he fired.

The gas tank on one of the trucks exploded. He felt the heat on his back, felt himself pitched to the side. He rolled, losing the flares before he stopped against something large and soft.

It was one of the Iraqi soldiers. Reaching to push himself away, Mongoose felt the man's uniform. It was wet; he'd been so scared he'd peed himself.

Shuffling himself to his knees, Mongoose realized the man was dead. It wasn't piss, it was blood. His left hand was smeared with it.

He turned away, looking for the bandolier. The flare the Hogs had launched was still descending, but its light was becoming fitful. One or two men moved on the far side of the road. He heard crying. His own arm hurt so bad he couldn't be entirely sure the moans weren't his own.

He saw his flares and pushed his body down for them as if he were a snake, not a man, curling in the cold fog and fine dirt. He made an effort to keep his right hand close to his body and immobile, but firing the flares was more important; he grappled with the holder and the small gun, had to use his bad arm, might have screamed with the pain, but his head was swimming now with adrenaline and he managed somehow to push the jackhammering throb to one side. He rolled back on his haunches into a seated position, cradling the launcher on the ground, and fired.

Nothing happened. He started to move his head forward to take a look when the rocket hissed upward, streaking toward the sky like a July 4th firework. Shocked, he jerked backward, dropped the launcher, and fell onto his back as the rocket whisked into the sky. The flare climbed quickly to nearly six hundred feet, where its small warhead ignited with a red burst.

Did they see it? The LUU-2 was still burning, and now there were other flares just north of them, decoys probably; whoever was flying the Hogs was worried about ground missiles.

They hadn't seen him. He would have to fire another. Mongoose scooped up the bandolier and forced it into his right hand. His fingers had numbed, but he managed to hold it steady enough to remove another of the small, cylindrical metal cartridges. There were like mini-thermoses, filled not with water but life-giving fire.

"No," said a voice behind him.

Mongoose turned and saw the Iraqi major, his pistol aimed at his face. The man's uniform was singed and tattered; fog and smoke swirled around him. But his mouth and eyes looked calm and determined despite the chaos.

"If you try to fire another flare, major, I will kill you. Put the launcher down."

The jets had moved off. Their engine noise was gone; they'd missed him.

"Put the launcher down. Now, Major. I will not tell you again."

Slowly, carefully, Mongoose complied.

47

Colonel Knowlington pushed the stick hard, felt the world drop away. His brain split into two halves. One contained the fuzzy TVM image, and the other the blur of dark earth in front of the Warthog's nose. He wanted to be low so there was no question that Mongoose would hear them. He wanted to make this fast, just in case someone other than his pilot was down there.

He also wanted not to plow into the earth.

But he worked the roll and dive well, pushing the plane over and then around and into a majestic swoop as pretty as poetry, pulling out and starting to recover just as the altimeter touched two hundred feet. He rocked across the path he'd mapped above as perfectly as if he were drawing it on paper.

The TVM was blank. The dirt here was cold and dead, without so much as an old log on the surface. He pushed around, checked his altitude, checked the screen, looked outside. Nothing.

The Warthog loved it down here. She felt like a horse finally released from the paddock.

Most likely, Shotgun hadn't meant the flares as a vote of no-confidence.

Knowlington nudged the Hog into another turn. He made four more low-level circuits, scanning the entire area as carefully as a miner working an old stream.

The TVM stayed blank. He couldn't get the shadow back, not even a hint of one.

"See anything?" he asked his wingman.

"Negative. I was hoping for a strobe, but nada."

"I'm going to do it again."

"Gotcha."

He got his airspeed down even further for the second low-level pass, dropping down toward two hundred knots. Plane didn't seem to mind; she seemed capable of just about stopping in midair.

He knew Mongoose wasn't here, but he made a complete circuit anyway. Where the hell could he be?

Most likely, the Iraqis had gotten him already. That explained why there were no radio transmissions.

There was another explanation. The pilot's body could be lying back there in the wreckage, mangled beyond recognition. They could be wasting their time, and risking their own necks.

He was going to catch holy shit when the brass found out about this little adventure. It'd be worth it if he came back with Mongoose.

What the hell. At his age, the only thing he was really good for was getting yelled at.

No. He could still fly. Damn Hog proved that. For all the bad things he'd once said about her, she didn't hold even the barest of grudges. She might be smirking a little bit, just around the edges, but otherwise she did what he asked, real smooth and professional.

Knowlington began pulling up as he returned to his starting point. This time Shotgun asked him if he'd seen anything.

"Negative," Skull told him. "Maybe that shadow wasn't anything, or maybe he heard all the commotion and started heading north. Let me come up a bit and then let's follow the highway."

"Gotcha."

"Say, Shotgun, I have a question for you. Is that music I hear behind your transmissions?"

"The Boss. Bruce Springsteen."

Knowlington snorted into his mike. "You planning on blasting the Iraqis with it?"

"I told Clyston it would be a good idea," said Shotgun. There was no question he was serious. "A couple of speakers mounted below the wings and I could scare the piss out of them while I was taking a bomb run. Like a Stuka's siren. That's what I'm talking about."

Hog drivers.

But hell, Knowlington thought, I'm one of them.

"Don't let it break your concentration," he told his wingman, fixing his eyes back on the TVM as he swung onto the new course.

48

His arm hurt like all hell. The pain seemed to push his whole body off at a strange angle, twisting his movements into a tortured caricature as the various muscles and nerves tried to compensate for the imbalance the injury had caused.

Mongoose had sprained his wrist twice in high school playing football, but this was a million times worse. His stomach felt as if he'd swallowed a bowling ball, and his temples were cold and sweaty. It might be because he was tired and hungry and thirsty, drained from the ordeal of the last twenty-four hours, or maybe it was just the way broken bones felt. He sat with his head against his knees, eyes closed, as the Iraqi major surveyed the remains of his command. The bandolier with its flares was only a few yards away, but it might as well be miles now. Mongoose mouthed a piece of his flight suit into his teeth, gritting against it as if it might offer some sort of relief.

"Your arm," said the Iraqi, standing over him. "What happened?"

"When I fell off the truck. It broke, I guess."

"Your friends did that to you."

He didn't answer. The major didn't know how right he

was. The attackers had definitely been Hogs, and they must have been looking for him. He would bet anything that Shotgun had been one of the pilots.

Pretty damn ironic.

"My division headquarters will send troops to pick us up. You will not escape."

Mongoose nudged his head back toward his knee, bit again. The ground was tilted to his left, then keeled over on its axis.

He wondered how long he could remain conscious.

"All right, Major, let us move back to the road. Come on now, get up."

Mongoose flinched when the man touched him under the shoulder, but once again his grip was light, not quite gentle but not wrenching either. Mongoose stumbled a little, aware that the captain had his pistol drawn.

"Go ahead of the trucks. I am right behind you."

Mongoose began to walk. They were alone. Four or five bodies were scattered near the truck, including that of the man he had landed against when the gas tank exploded.

There had been at least a half-dozen more, but they were nowhere around. It was possible they were biding their time in a defensive position up the road, or had regrouped with an NCO. But Mongoose didn't think so; he thought they had run off. They were mostly kids, after all, and it was a good chance that this had been their first real combat.

He'd heard a lot of things before the war about how tough the Iraqis were; the country had sustained a long conflict with Iran, after all. But the Iraqis didn't seem to be living up to their advance billing.

"Ahead of the truck and onto the road," said the major. "Keep moving."

Mongoose corrected his course. Walking along the highway had its advantages; it would make it easier for the Hogs to find him.

They'd be back soon. The sun was starting to peek up at the far edge of the horizon. They'd have an easy time spotting him once it was light.

What would the major do then?

Shoot him most likely.

They walked together for no more than five minutes, Mongoose leading the way slowly, holding his damaged right arm but not looking at it.

"Stop now. We'll rest here. Let me see your arm."

"It's fine," Mongoose told him.

"Let me see it," said the Iraqi. He held his pistol in his left hand, close to his body. Mongoose eyed it, thought of trying to wrestle for it. The Iraqi didn't seem particularly powerful, but of course Johnson had only one good arm. And the man was too far away; he'd get off at least two shots before Mongoose even come close.

Bile welled in his throat as he held his right arm out. If he'd had anything in his stomach besides water, he would have puked.

"Undo your shirtsleeve. This is as close as I'm getting."

As Mongoose reached to his sleeve, he realized it was covered with blood. His first thought was that the blood had come from the Iraqi he'd stumbled over earlier, but as he curled his fingers beneath the cuff, he realized it was wetter beneath the sleeve. The involuntary reaction sent a fresh wave of nausea and pain through his body. He dropped his arm with a groan and sank slowly, finally overwhelmed. Everything beyond the immediate confines of his body disappeared into a hazy buzz.

"Do not move," said the Iraqi from inside the haze. Mongoose felt the barrel of the pistol against his cheek. A knife appeared at his sleeve, and he felt the fabric being torn away. The pain he felt in his arm made Mongoose shriek. He stumbled against the Iraqi, then cringed, his eyes closed, expecting the man to shoot him.

But he did not. The Iraqi waited for Mongoose to catch his balance with his good arm, then calmly took two steps backwards. He slipped the knife back into its sheath.

"You have a compound fracture. It will have to be set as soon as we get back. There will be a doctor. Just be sure to say that I did not do that to you when we reach my headquarters."

Mongoose stuttered a yes. The buzz began to subside, the pain receding or his ability to deal with it growing. He leaned back from his three-point stance, resting in a crouch.

It seemed inconceivable that the Iraqi officer would be this kind. Surely, if their situations had been reversed and his own men were lying dead nearby, at least some of his anger would have shown through. He might even have shot the son of a bitch. No one would blame him, and he could always say the guy was trying to escape.

If anyone even bothered to ask.

Maybe it was a duty thing, the major under orders to fetch the pilot back alive. Maybe there was a reward, and it would only be paid if he was unharmed. Still, to act so mildly toward him—it seemed incredible.

And yet the Iraqi was the enemy, not a friend. He had meant it when he said he would shoot him if he tried to escape; there seemed no doubt about that.

"I'm going to put a canteen on the ground. When I step back, you can have a drink."

"Thank you, Major."

"You're welcome, Major."

Mongoose focused his eyes on the ground in front of him, waiting for the canteen. His tongue was dry in his mouth, brittle; he wanted water so badly, his heart started pounding.

It could be a trick, he thought when the canteen failed to appear. Maybe perverted revenge.

But no, the Iraqi had only been unscrewing the top. He stepped back and motioned for Mongoose to come forward.

The water tasted incredibly delicious. He knew he shouldn't have too much—more than a few mouthfuls on an empty, parched stomach and it would all come shooting back, leaving him more dehydrated than before. But it took great effort to stop. He squatted with the canteen between his legs and fixed the cap with his good hand.

"Very creative," said the Iraqi after retrieving the canteen. "You must have been a good engineer."

"Actually, I probably sucked. All I've ever really wanted to do was fly. Engineering was just a backup."

"Too bad you didn't choose it," said the Iraqi.

"I've done all right."

As Mongoose finally rose, a fresh breeze scratched at his

face. He didn't feel its chill; instead, it seemed to push more of the pain away.

He remembered Kathy's letter, and reached for it involuntarily.

"Stop!" demanded the Iraqi.

"It's nothing. Just the letter you gave me back before. From my wife. I just thought of her."

It was too dark to read his face clearly, but the enemy officer's tone said that he would no longer completely trust him. "Empty your pocket slowly," the Iraqi told him.

Mongoose reached inside and took out the letter. He held it up.

"Just the letter from my wife. It's not worth anything to you. You already saw it and gave it back."

They were silent for a moment. The Iraqi reached forward to grab the letter, and Mongoose felt anger well up inside him. For a half second he thought he was going to dive into the man; his muscles tensed for what would have been a quick, suicidal fight.

Then the Iraqi snatched the letter from his hand and jumped back. Any chance of attacking him was gone.

"I haven't read it yet," said Mongoose.

"You'll have plenty of time later. Let's find something to make a sling," said the Iraqi. "And then we will walk. It is better than sitting around waiting for your friends to come back, don't you think?"

49

Skull snapped the mike button as he acknowledged the airborne controller. Things were getting busy, but even with upwards of a hundred pilots trucking north, no one had heard from Mongoose or picked up his emergency beacon.

The ground had an orange glow to it, and some pieces of vegetation near the horizon looked as if they were on fire. The buildings were dull black and silver, just starting to catch the light.

The wrecked overpass and its assorted debris came up on his right wing. Skull walked past it, his indicated airspeed down below 200 knots—he could flop down the landing gear and put down on the roadway. Skull gave himself more throttle and took the Hog into a gentle climb, gradually working himself into a wide, lazy turn—considering where they were, it was lazy—while he scanned the ground for any sign of Mongoose or his parachute. It ought to be visible by now.

Assuming he'd gone out.

Skull gave a quick glance at the gas gauge on his right panel, then put his eyes back outside, moving ahead toward the wreckage of the A-10A, working out what had happened for the third or fourth time.

He was hit back there, the plane crashed up here. Some-where in between, there ought to be a chute.

Or his seat at least, if everything screwed up.

Nothing.

Okay, so there's a lot of wind. Still, he didn't just dis-appear.

Mongoose kept the Hog climbing as he circled again, his eyes working the ground like a miner sifting for gold. Shotgun had done all of this yesterday, the F-16's had done this—nothing.

What if the Iraqis had picked him up right away? That would explain why there was no radio transmission. They might have taken the chute and seat. Most likely they would, either as evidence or souvenirs.

Passing over the Scuds, Skull reset the attack run that had gotten Mongoose nailed. Devil One was there, Devil Two there. Overpass was immense, got to give them that. Attack here, zoom in. Bam, bam, bam. Mongoose pulls up.

His head is still back with the front of the underpass, wondering why the hell he didn't get a bigger boom. Maybe he's figured out they're decoys.

There's no warning until the launch. The gunner must be using his eyeballs, or something is screwed up.

Using his eyeballs? Shit. What the hell would the odds be on making that shot?

But something like that happened. The ECMs are useless against the Roland anyway. So let's say the gunner lets go and the missile takes up its own targeting. Mongoose starts pulling off here when he's hit.

Okay, no, he didn't quite make the turn. Which actually gives him this vector when the Roland comes out.

Yes, and the Hog kicked due north after the ejection—okay, he was going this way when he went out.

Mongoose has turned off, he'd be working himself back, momentum shifting around. Doesn't see the shot.

Which hits him here? How?

No. He's still moving. Has to be back over there, because otherwise he wouldn't have gotten both trailers before he pulled off. But boy, this really doesn't line up with the crash site.

Of course it doesn't, because the missile takes out part of the wing, enough to make it spin back.

The plane was throwing them off. Damn, he knew from Nam you couldn't trust the stinking wreckage. Planes had a mind of their own once no one was watching them. Hell, he'd heard of one flew all the way back to its aircraft carrier and landed on its own.

Probably not a true story.

So Mongoose is fighting a yawl and leaning over like a sinking ship when he pulls the handles. Comes out like an artillery shot instead of a mortar, sideways.

And then you add the wind.

He was further south than they'd been looking.

Much. Beyond where they'd smoked those trucks.

Shit.

"Shotgun, were you inverted when you saw Mongoose?"

"I was climbing."

"Put your plane there."

"The exact spot?"

"As close as you can. Slow it down."

"I go any slower I'm gong to be moving backwards."

"Hogs can't do that?"

The colonel watched Devil Two fly over the dead truck, then jerk upwards and around. "Saw it here out of the corner of my eye."

"You sure you weren't farther south?"

"I might've been a little. My angle was sharper, that's for sure. I saw him while I was jinking."

"And he got both Scud decoys on his run?"

"Smoked 'em."

"Take my wing."

"What are you doing?"

"Just crank up your music and follow me."

50

When the Iraqi major was sure the soldier was dead, he knelt near him and with his knife cut away a piece of his shirt. He worked roughly, keeping one eye on Mongoose the entire time. He knotted the strip of cloth with his teeth, then flung it toward the pilot.

The sling landed on the ground. Mongoose waited for the major to step back, then took a step and scooped it up.

He caught a strong whiff of the dead man's sweat as he pulled it around his shoulder.

The pain had leveled off. He eased his arm into the sling, then pressed his fingers into a fist around the edge of the material. They were limp and starting to swell slightly.

"And now we start walking," said the Iraqi. "You first."

Mongoose turned and started toward the road. The sun was nearly up now. He knew the Hogs would come back; it was just a question of waiting long enough for them.

Had the Iraqi been lying about the soldiers coming for them? No matter; the Hogs would smoke them as they'd smoked the trucks.

They might smoke *him* too. He'd have to wave a flag or something.

How?

If the planes appeared, he might be able to convince the Iraqi to surrender with him. Maybe that was why he was treating him so well—maybe the Iraqi hoped an SAR team would pop up over the horizon.

He'd been trained as an engineer in America. Maybe he wanted to go back.

That was why he was being so nice.

"You're going slow," said the Iraqi. He sounded like he was ten feet behind him.

"I'm tired."

"You'll sleep soon enough."

"What happened to the rest of your men? The planes didn't kill them all."

A sore point obviously—the Iraqi major didn't answer right away. When he did, his voice was sharp and stern.

"That is not your concern."

They walked more. Mongoose's legs were starting to wear out, but his head raced with pain and adrenaline. He needed some plan to get away, but his mind wouldn't focus long enough on any one possibility. Run for it, turn around and overpower the Iraqi, talk his captor into giving up with him—ideas flitted indiscriminately through his brain, each as likely as the next. He had no more judgment.

"Why have you stopped?" the Iraqi asked him.

"I'm stopped?"

Mongoose turned around, genuinely surprised. They were still near the trucks. He hadn't gone more than a few yards. The sky had lightened sufficiently now that they could see each other's expressions from ten paces away, and the major must have realized that his prisoner was not trying to trick him.

"We cannot stop. You may be too tired to keep moving," the Iraqi told him.

"I'm really tired. I've been up since very early yesterday."

"If you cannot come with me, I'll kill you. I'll say that the planes did it, or that you were trying to escape."

"My legs feel like they're going to fall off. Let me sit a

moment, then I'll try again. Or we can wait for the men you said were coming for us."

Reluctantly, the Iraqi motioned that he could rest. Jangled as he slipped down, Mongoose's arm screamed with pain. In a way, he welcomed it—the Iraqi was right; he was dangerously close to falling asleep.

Not even sleep, oblivion. His body had been through so much in the past twenty-four hours, in the past week, since the war began, in the past two months—he just didn't have anything left. Sleep was a warm, beckoning sauna, waiting to sweat the fatigue from his body.

He had to survive. Sleep was as much the enemy, more the enemy, than the Iraqi major.

"Why did you leave the States?" Mongoose asked.

"I told you. I came home," said the Iraqi. He lit a cigarette and inhaled deeply, savoring the nicotine.

"You married?"

"Yes. I have two children."

"I just had my first. I was there when he was born. Pretty intense."

The Iraqi took another long drag of his cigarette. He held his pistol straight down in his hand; it was a dull shadow against his leg.

"What are their names?" Mongoose asked the Iraqi.

"Names?"

"Your kids?"

"Amir and Sohrab. Boys."

"Mine's Robert. Robby. He's three months old. Or three and a half by now. Almost four."

The Iraqi didn't answer. Maybe he was tired too, or maybe he was thinking about the men who'd deserted him.

Or the ones lying dead nearby.

I'm going to have to kill him, Mongoose realized. *He's not going to let me go when the Hogs come back. And he's not going to surrender.*

"Come on," said the Iraqi. "Let's move."

"Won't your headquarters people be coming soon? Can't we just wait?"

"It's better for you to walk. You have to keep blood circulating. Besides, you may go into shock."

"I already am." Mongoose tried to laugh.

"I don't think so."

"You a doctor?"

"I took an EMT class at the college."

"Why'd you go to America for school if you were coming home?"

"I wasn't coming home then." The Iraqi took one more serious breath from the cigarette, burning it down to its filter. He flicked it away just as the ember reached his fingertips. "I wanted to be an American."

"Why?"

"I wanted to be rich. Come on, let's go."

"Are you going to give me back my letter?"

"Up!"

Mongoose's legs were so stiff he had trouble getting up. The ligaments in his knee had stiffened; the pain wasn't much compared to his arm, but with the fatigue now it slowed him even further. The major was right—he had to keep moving or his muscles would just shut down.

"So I guess you didn't get rich," he told his captor as he started to walk.

"There are more important things."

Maybe he didn't shoot me because there are no bullets in his gun.

Mongoose had heard stories of troops not being issued ammunition for fear that they would revolt against Saddam. But were those stories true? And would an officer not be given ammunition?

Why else would he let me live? Because he's a nice guy? Because it was his duty to bring me back alive.

"You're walking much too slowly," said the Iraqi.

"I'm sorry. Everything's tightening up on me. I slammed my knee when I parachuted. My body feels like it's paralyzed. And my damn head is pounding like a jackhammer. Back of my neck."

"Keep moving. It's the best thing."

"I'm trying. What made you change your mind?"

"About what?"

"About coming back here."

The Iraqi didn't answer.

"My son was born three months ago," said Mongoose. Talking felt like taking a long sip of a very sweet drink, something sappier than a margarita. He was in shock, definitely. And he was so tired his mind was drifting into a dreamy unreality. He felt as if he might be on the verge of hallucinating. He felt as if he might be on the verge of dying.

And he had to kill this man if he was going to be rescued.

"I was there for his birth," Mongoose said, feeling each thread of his consciousness slipping away.

"What was it like?" the Iraqi asked.

What was it like?

Like something beyond comprehension. Standing there, seeing his son's head inching out, then all of a sudden bolting, almost flying forward.

Holding the baby, warm and sticky.

"I don't know if I can describe it," Mongoose told him. "It was very surreal."

As surreal as now, standing stock-still in the middle of the Iraqi desert with a man who had a gun a few feet from his chest, pointed at the ground but easily raised?

It had to be empty or he'd be dead already.

Maybe not. But he'd never get the Iraqi to let him go or join him. For all the kindness he had shown, he had to be killed.

No. If he could overpower him, he could just leave him here, make him walk away.

But what made him think they were coming back? By now the Air Force had probably concluded Mongoose was dead. They'd have seen the wreckage and not heard a radio. The Hogs had probably greased the trucks out of frustration and anger. They were mad because they had to give him up.

"I would have liked to see the birth of one of my children," said the Iraqi.

"Maybe you will. The next one. Could I have some water? I really need a drink."

The Iraqi reached to his belt for his canteen.

Now, Mongoose's brain said. Now is your last chance. Jump him.

By the time he told himself it was a foolish move, he was already rolling on top of the enemy.

51

Kathy was so drained she went to bed after talking to the reporters. She began drifting off right away, but then something stalled—her mind stuck and she couldn't get to sleep. She lay under the blankets, thoughts plowing back and forth in her brain.

There had been plenty of sleepless nights over the past two months, and not because of the baby. Robby was really perfect.

What would it be like raising him alone? A boy without a father.

Kathy wrapped the blanket tighter around her shoulder, pushing herself against the bed. It was nearly impossible to clear her mind of those thoughts. Most of the tricks she used to get to sleep—thinking about good times in the past, or to come—just brought her husband back sharply.

She tried thinking of Paris. They'd never been there, but they had talked about going. If they had had a real honeymoon, that was where they would have gone.

When they had a real honeymoon. Jimmy had promised they would go soon. He had leave coming up, and there was a little bit of money saved, and hell, why not charge the credit cards up like everyone else.

Kathy rolled herself out from under the covers and sat on the edge of the bed for a second, wondering whether she should just get up and get dressed, maybe have some coffee or even a cigarette with the others.

She could hear her father-in-law's voice in the kitchen. It sounded a little like her husband's.

Jimmy's was a little deeper. His words came quicker.

It had been ages since they'd talked. Ages since they'd last slept together. It had been in this bed. Her back and legs and arms ached to feel him curled around them.

She thought she heard the baby stirring. Kathy got up and took two steps, peeked over. He lay on his back with his eyes closed, mouth open, arms casually flung apart.

A perfect little boy. She reached down and though he was sleeping, picked him up and held him tight against her chest.

52

The man felt less substantial than he expected, his body lighter, thinner, yet he struggled viciously, writhing and snaking below Mongoose's.

It was all or nothing. The Iraqi's gun was surely empty, but the man would pound him with his bare hands if he won, kick him into unconsciousness, and then go back and get one of his soldier's guns. Mongoose fought despite the pain, flailing and shaking and punching and rolling, butting his head into his captor's chest, working his legs and knees as if they were battering rams. Every cell in his body flared with inhuman anger. He heard himself screaming, felt himself being pushed over, bulled his shoulders and screamed again.

The gun was in his chest, between them. The Iraqi was screaming too.

"I'll let you go!" Mongoose yelled. "I'll let you live because you let me live, but I'm escaping! I'm living!"

They rolled over twice. Pain was his whole body. He'd never known a time when he wasn't pain. Mongoose kicked and crashed his head into his captor's chin, felt the groan.

Fingers clawed at his eye. A nail gouged at the corner,

burrowing into the edge of his nose. Fog and dirt and sweat and sand swirled through their bodies, consuming them with a fine, misty crud.

The gun was between them. Mongoose felt its barrel against his chest.

"I'll let you go!" he told the major. "I'll let you go, but my guys are coming back and I'm going with them!"

There was an explosion, and the pain that had taken over his body disappeared. The air turned to metal and hung in his nose.

The Iraqi let go of him. Dazed, Mongoose slipped backwards, lay on the ground a good while. The sky was lightening. It was dawn.

"I meant it," he told the Iraqi, sitting up. "My guys are coming back. You can come with me if you want."

Mongoose looked over and saw the major's body prone on the ground, a large, black and red oozing hole covering three fourths of his throat.

53

Shotgun pushed the plane to follow his boss.

Thing was, Knowlington was a different guy in the air. Not a bad guy, a good flier definitely, but different.

He was quicker with his words, and used a hell of a lot less of them.

Plus, on the ground he let people toss their ideas in. Up here, wham-bam, this is what we're doing. Follow along and keep your lip zipped.

And your cockpit music turned down.

Not that Shotgun was the sensitive type. And hell, the old coot knew what he was doing, even if they were flying a good ten miles south of where Shotgun was sure Mongoose had gone out.

The pilot shifted in the seat, feeling himself into a good position. One of these days he was going to figure out how to get some sort of form-fitting thing going on. You couldn't use a thicker cushion; the ejection force was so severe the metal base would slam up through a pad and hit you harder than a bullet. Still, there ought to be some way of making the frame itself more comfortable. Kind of thing was done all the time; all it took was creative customization. Maybe ol' Tinman could handle it. Guy had a way with metal.

Shotgun stretched his neck, working against a kink. His eyes slid around the Hog's panels, making sure the numbers agreed with his gut. They did.

The idea to use the Mavericks was a damn good one. Hell, they should have found Mongoose by now.

Not that he wanted to think about that too much. He decided it was probably not a bad time for a Twinkie. Except that he didn't have any left.

Have to go to the backup chocolate Twizzlers in his leg pack.

Shotgun slipped his hand down toward the pocket's zipper and retrieved the bag of candy. One thing about war—you could never ever get enough licorice.

The colonel was already pushing his Hog into the bushes as Shotgun finished wadding the Twizzlers into his mouth. They were near the trucks they'd splashed on the way north before dawn. He could see them in the foggy haze, ghost trucks haunted by dead men.

Something was moving down there.

No way it could be anything but an Iraqi soldier, right? Shit.

He gripped his stick tightly and leaned forward, his plane a dark green angel streaking toward the earth.

54

His eyes were open. They were a small part of the face, with brown irises glossy in the growing blue light.

The final trace of surprise lingered in the cheeks.

Mongoose did not want to touch the body, but he could not leave Kathy's letter in the dead man's pocket. He knelt, feeling his joints crack; suddenly dizzy, he reached out to steady himself and put his hand on the dead Iraqi's chest.

The letter. I have to get the letter.

He fumbled with the button on the major's shirt pocket. His chest was still warm.

The wrong pocket. He removed his hand as if he'd felt a scorpion, undid the other button, grabbed the folded envelope.

Something else slipped out of the pocket. He could tell from the slick backing that it was a photograph. Mongoose bolted upright and began running away, back toward the burned-out shells of the trucks the A-10As had smoked.

He didn't get very far before finding himself almost out of breath. He told himself to relax, told himself he'd be rescued soon. He needed to get into checklist mode.

Checklist mode. First item—make sure the rest of these bastards are all dead.

He needed a weapon. The closest body was about a hundred yards away, at the edge of the road. The man's rifle lay in his outstretched hand.

Dead? Or was he just pretending, waiting until the American dropped his guard?

Mongoose stopped, edged to his left, off the highway. He froze, scanning beyond the man for any movement.

Nothing.

He edged out further. The ground had a good layer of dust on it, but was hard-packed. He could step easily. It wasn't like walking on a beach, with all its loose sand.

For just a second, he smelled salt water in his nostrils.

Checklist mode.

The Iraqi wasn't moving, but something beyond him was. Mongoose pushed his legs and his lungs, started walking, heart pounding. His muscles were stiff, but they seemed to move easier the faster he went.

It was a Russian rifle, an assault gun. Mongoose snatched at it, ready to pry it from the man's hand, but it came up so quickly he nearly fell over.

Something was moving near the far truck. One of the bodies.

He pushed the gun up, cradling it against his ribs, and squeezed the trigger, expecting a torrent of bullets. Nothing happened.

The body kept moving. It was coming toward him.

He looked at the unfamiliar rifle in his hand. The gun had a cocking handle on the right side.

Pull it back? Push it?

He had to steady the gun with his legs to get at the handle. He pulled it back, looked up, and saw the Iraqi soldier less than twenty yards away, just reaching for a rifle.

He pulled up the gun and pulled the trigger again. The rifle barked ferociously, the ground ahead of the man erupting with bullets. For all the noise, the backlash from the gun was mild, no more than that from a .22 squirrel plinker.

But he missed. And now the soldier had reached the gun.

Mongoose felt his legs go out from under him—he landed on his butt and rolled, his bad arm screaming.

Was he cocked? Did he have to reload?

Desperate, his finger flailed for the lever, reached back for the trigger. He heard gunfire, but realized it was the other man shooting, not him. Finally, bullets began spitting from his gun. He pushed the barrel up and then over into the cloudy haze of the man, pressed his finger until he realized nothing more was coming out and the soldier had stopped moving.

Mongoose used the rifle to get back to his feet. It slipped from his hands as he got up, and he let it fall; it was empty and no good to him now. He walked as quickly as he could to the man he'd just killed. He kicked him to make sure he was dead, kicked the gun away.

Maybe I ought to pray, he thought. *Or better, play the lottery. Because I sure as hell have been one lucky son of a bitch. All these bastards lying around me, and I'm the only one left. God damn, I am one lucky son of a bitch.*

The low whoosh of an approaching jet brought him back to reality. He stopped for a second, listening, realizing it was a Hog, knowing it must be one of his companions.

And he had no way to signal them. They were still some distance off, low enough for him to hear. They'd skim the trucks and think he was an Iraqi.

Or worse, they'd miss him altogether.

He'd dropped his flares somewhere around here. A desperate frenzy seized his brain as he trotted around, looking for them. Shadows and hallucinations poked at the corners of his vision, as if the dead were coming back to life, as if he were caught in the middle of a horror film. He tried to hold it all away, to stay in checklist mode. It wasn't going to get him. He was too goddamn lucky for it to get him.

Too many people were counting on him. The squadron. Kath. Robby.

He saw something in the dust, the bandolier. He ran for it, tripped, stretched his arm out.

Not the bandolier but a jacket, crusted with blood.

It was impossible to get to his feet. He could hear the

planes getting closer, overhead. They'd leave. This would
be his last chance.

The ground felt so damn good. Sleep.

Mongoose pushed to his knee, clawed at the earth. He
finally reached his feet.

The bandolier and the small flashlight-like flare gun lay a
short distance away. It seemed to glow, catching the glint of
the hidden sun. The wind kicked up and sprayed dust in his
face, bits and pieces of debris clinging to his chest and face.
He tried brushing them off with his good hand, waving at
the air as if a swarm of flies had appeared to harass him.

As he flailed, Mongoose realized something had stuck to
his pants leg. It was a piece of paper, glued there by blood.
He pulled it off and started to throw it aside, before realizing
what it was.

The dead Iraqi major's photograph.

He pushed it into the fist of his wounded hand.

The bandolier was at his feet. He knelt and scooped it up.

His fingers fumbled with the launcher as his mind began
to float above his body, moving over the ground, far away
to a place where he didn't have to be lucky and blessed or
just another sucker about to be done in by the most ironic
ending Fate could imagine.

55

Even before he saw the flare, Skull knew Mongoose was here. Call it intuition or ESP or stubbornness or just dumb luck, he knew his guy was there.

He wasn't sure, though, whether he was still alive. Anybody could fire a flare. It would be a perfect way to lure them close enough for a good shoulder-launched missile.

There was only one way to find out. And it wasn't a job he could give a subordinate.

A flicker of fear shot through the fingers of his left hand as he steadied the throttle.

Good, he thought. I can deal with that.

"Watch for a ground launch," he told Shotgun.

"I got it."

Low and slow. Dangerous as hell, but there was no substitute. The flaps were out as air brakes, he was nearly going backwards, damn it, but he couldn't tell. There wasn't enough light and he was too far off.

And his eyes were failing him. That was the real story. He was old.

There were bodies, but none seemed to be moving.

Someone had fired the flares. He was going to call the search-and-rescue team in.

Hell, it was either that or land the plane.

"See him?" asked Shotgun as he pulled up.

"I saw someone. I'm coming around again."

"Go for it. I'm on you."

He came in even lower and slower than he had the first time, but the truth was, he was still moving too damn fast for his eyes.

Bodies were strewn haphazardly. He couldn't tell if one was wearing a flight suit, if one was different than the rest.

He couldn't tell whether they were all dead. Nothing had moved.

But hell—he knew Mongoose was down there. The flare had definitely been one of theirs.

Skull refused to consider any other possibility. The only thing he worried about now was bringing the helicopter into an ambush.

But wouldn't anybody looking to grease an American take him out? Ducks flew slower than he did.

Another shot of fear in his fingers. Skull turned the Warthog around for a third circuit. This time, he wasn't looking at the ground. Instead, he concentrated on holding the plane a half knot over stall speed as he made his tail as fat a target as possible.

A water pistol could have nailed him.

"Mark the location so we both have it," said Skull. "I'm calling in the helos."

"Kick ass."

A pair of Special Ops Pave Low helicopters, call signs Big Bear and Little Bear, had been waiting not far from the border to make the pickup. But it was going to take them and their escorts at least a half hour to get here.

"We'll wait," Skull told the controller.

The rescue choppers were part of a full-blown "package" or group of airplanes that undertook rescues behind the lines. F-15 Eagles were tasked for combat air patrol, Weasels were watching for SAMS, a fresh pair of A-10As flew close support escorting the choppers in, tankers were available to keep everyone topped off—combat might come down to one-on-one, but there were a ton of guys and gals behind the scenes making it happen. Part of Colonel Knowlington's brain mapped the different elements out as if on a dry-erase board, plotting and planning like a squadron commander.

The other part focused on the desert, scanning the ground for possible resistance.

Two halves, commander and pilot. The pilot was the younger, more primitive Knowlington—the one with better reflexes and a cast-iron gut. He was damn sure Mongoose was down there, and alive.

The commander wasn't quite so positive. Sure be nice if one of the bodies down there got up and started doing a jumping jack or something.

The two Hogs patrolled the area in a large orbit at about eight thousand feet, giving themselves a decent vantage to check for movement on the roads. There had been none in the five minutes or so since Skull had called for the pickup.

"Looking at a dust bunny comin' out of the north," said Shotgun. "Shit. Something's heading down the road, beyond the buildings."

Skull immediately cut short his leg of the circle and the two planes winged into a combat trail, Shotgun offset on the right side of the lead and back a half mile.

"Let's bring this out to the west, then take a fast turn to head back," said Skull. "I don't want to billboard Mongoose's location."

"Gotcha."

"Take it up to fifteen, give us a little more margin for error." He quick-checked his instruments as the Hog began climbing, making sure he was ready for action. He considered calling for reinforcements, but decided to hold off until he knew what they were up against. The helicopters were still a good ways off, and Shotgun's dust bunny might turn out to be a jeep dragging a fender—he still hadn't spotted it.

Even without a lot of ordnance to weigh her down, the Hog took its time going uphill. Take an Eagle and put her nose at the sun and bam, she was there. Same with an F-16.

Thud could climb with the best of them, unless she had a full load. Even then she could go like all hell. The Pratt & Whitney J75 turbojet was a brand-new engine at the time, with huge thrust—nearly 25,000 pounds in afterburner, which could carry the plane over Mach 2. A bear and a half to service, and from the early days there were problems with the autopilot and the computer and the fire-control system. But damn, he loved to fly the Thunderchief, a lot more than the Phantom. They said the F-4 was a better plane, but you couldn't prove it by him.

He'd had his worst days in a Phantom.

Leaving his wingman. Chickened out.

Negated everything else.

"Looks like there's a whole convoy or something. Be almost nine o'clock, north there."

For just a second the voice sounded unfamiliar, as if Skull had been expecting Bear to be talking to him from the backseat.

"How the hell did you see that through the ground fog and all?" he asked Shotgun when he finally spotted it. He took the Hog further east, pushing to come at the convoy from the side. "All I see's dust."

"Got X-ray eyes," said Shotgun.

The airborne controller checked in with the SAR helicopter's time to pickup—twenty minutes. By the time Skull acknowledged, he was close enough to Shotgun's dust bunny to see that it wasn't a jeep.

Or rather, it wasn't just a jeep. There were at least two dozen vehicles on the road. They were moving fast, in the direction of their flier. Skull was up to ten thousand feet, flying a bit slow but in a reasonable position for a Maverick attack. He kept coming, deciding to make his approach angle as steep as possible.

"Looks like we're going to have to smoke these guys," he told Shotgun.

"Hot damn."

"They must think Mongoose is the fucking President. All right, we freeze the column first. I take the lead truck and whatever else I can get at the head. Put your cluster bombs about a third of the way back if you can. Shit, they may see us—column's starting to break up."

The AWACS controller broke in before Shotgun could acknowledge. "Devil Flight, snap one-eighty. Snap one-eighty."

It was a dire warning to take evasive maneuvers by jumping quickly to a new course—enemy interceptors were coming for them.

Ordinarily, Skull would have complied immediately. He was supposed to comply immediately; the warning was meant to save his plane and his life. Taking evasive action was the prudent thing to do.

But he wasn't being prudent. He was saving his guy. No way he was turning around and running for home with his tail between his legs, not this time.

He ignored the controller.

The AWACS, with its powerful radar, knew instantly that its order had not been followed.

"Devil Leader. This is Abracadabra. We have a pair of MiGs taking off from Al Nassiriya. Take evasive action."

"Noted," Skull told the controller. He didn't bother communicating with Shotgun; he knew he would stay with him.

"Repeat?" asked the AWACS.

"Noted. We are engaging a troop column approximately ten miles north of our pickup area."

"Devil Leader, the MiGs are off the field and are vectored in your direction. Snap one-eighty. Repeat, snap one-eighty!"

The first vehicle looked like some sort of armored personnel carrier, wheeled, not tracked. A good, easy target for a Maverick.

Even a greenhorn like him ought to be able to splash the damn thing. Problem was, he couldn't get the crosshair to move. And all of a sudden he was feeling disoriented, eyes not knowing where to look, TVM or windscreen.

Stick to the monitor, damn it.

The personnel carrier was fat in the middle of the targeting screen, and the cursor sat at the bottom. He switched from the narrow to wide and back to the narrow but better-magnified view, losing his target momentarily. He eased the plane's nose just a tad and had his target back, juicy and hot. And now the cursor had it right in the middle.

Didn't make sense, but hey, there it was.

"Devil Leader? The MiGs!"

"Noted," he told the controller, locking his cursor.

"Sir?"

"Noted!" he said, and in the same second the Maverick thumped off the wing, hiccuping in the air before her motor kicked into high gear.

56

The flak vest the sergeant had given him was way too big, and no matter how Dixon tried adjusting it, he couldn't get comfortable in it. For the Special Ops troops used to it, the gear was a lightweight second skin, but for him the damn thing felt more awkward than wearing a parka at a July Fourth picnic. He shifted under it and tried to get a fix through the window on where they were. They had come in over the border more than an hour ago, sitting here so they would be ready to grab their guy once he was found. As far as the air commandos were concerned, squatting in enemy territory was no more dangerous than waiting on line for a roller-coaster ride.

The chopper's massive turboshafts cranked with an immense fury; they didn't seem to lift off so much as vibrate forward, the big Pave Low rising gracefully. The Air Force crew chief emerged from the pilots' station and announced that they had a good fix on Major Johnson, even though his radio was out. Shouldn't be much of a problem snatching him from the jaws of death this time around.

The rest of the men, all well-versed in behind-the-lines

operations, grinned and rechecked their rifles. Most had been completely silent since Dixon came on board.

Iraq passed by ten feet below. The helicopter rushed forward with an angry beat, its powerful rotors churning the sky.

The pilot called back that they were ten minutes from their man. And there was a column of Iraqi Republican Guards racing them for him.

The sergeant chucked him on the shoulder. "No offense, sir, but you just hang back the first few seconds, make sure the area is secure before you go jumping out of the aircraft. Okay?"

"No sweat."

"Good." The sergeant stuck an M-16 in his hands. "It's loaded and ready to rock."

Dixon's stomach flipped over backwards as he grabbed the rifle.

"Thanks," he yelled.

"Don't mention it. But, uh, sir, again, no offense, but I'd be obliged if you didn't point it in my direction."

57

Skull edged the stick ever so slightly as he got ready to launch his second missile. The plane was right there, right with him, as tight to his body as anything, even his old Thud. Better than that really, and truer, without having to worry so much about your muscles giving out. He was well into his dive, coming steep as if he were dropping unguided munitions—old-school habits—but this wasn't a problem. He had the number-three truck dead-on. The pilot punched out the Maverick, then turned his attention back to his windscreen. His cannon was loaded and ready to chew. An armored personnel carrier rumbled into his aim, and he pushed the button on his stick. The force of the seven-barrel Gatling's ten-thousand-pound recoil seemed to hit him in the face, slamming his head back away from his eyes. His eyes didn't move because they were fixed on the HUD and windscreen, guiding the steady stream of metallic death into the metal. He still had altitude and a good angle as he found another APC toward the end of the line and squeezed the trigger for three short bursts. The bullets sliced through the front and then the top of the lightly armored personnel carrier as easily as if it were made of tin.

Skull let go of the trigger, and the plane bucked so sharply he thought he had flamed the engines. His stomach kicked some familiar juices up toward his chest and he realized the plane was fine. He lit the gun again, this time for a much quicker burst, lining up on a truck at the very end of the column, but missing. He was by it and pulling off, his rhythm back, heart pounding, and damn, it had been twenty-something years since this feeling of weightlessness and heartburn and adrenaline had wrecked his stomach, twenty-something years since the rubbery-plastic in his nose turned nauseous and the straps pushed against his chest like the restraints on an electric chair. He'd missed it badly, missed the smell of sulfur that somehow whipped into his nostrils, the suggestion of brimstone and Judgment he felt when dealing death to the enemy.

"We got flak coming up on your right wing," said Bear in his ear. "Coming off a second column. You see them?"

It wasn't Bear, it was Shotgun. And he was telling Knowlington that one of the tracked vehicles off to the flank of the main column was a self-propelled antiaircraft gun, the Zsu-23-4. But Skull's brain blurred, put him in his Phantom, put him back to the last time he was trying to protect a downed squadron mate. He saw the flash of the gun out of the corner of his eye, remembered the ridge in Laos.

The acid burned through into his lungs. They had a whole ridge of fire coming at them, unguided but a wall of lead and there was no way around it, just get the pedal to the metal because he was out of energy and as he nosed past the plane seemed to be in slow motion. He could hear Bear gasping for air through the open mike, trying to tell him something. His own mask was sucked up tight to his face, he was yanking the Phantom's stick and for one of the few times since learning how to land he was praying, realizing he actually might eat shit today.

An entire division's worth of antiaircraft guns. All set into the ridge. Shells were whizzing past unexploded, big shells, huge things, 57mm suckers that looked like streamlined piranha coming at him. Some moved fast and some moved slowly; all ran straight at him and there wasn't a damn thing he could do to get away from them except hang on tight.

It took maybe three seconds to clear the wall, no more than five seconds beyond that to push the airplane into a completely safe space. But the time passed like weeks, slower than the dark spot of a furball, the moment in a dogfight when the opponent is unsighted and quite probably behind you.

Bingo fuel, Bear was saying.

Bingo fuel. They'd been low on fuel even before the antiair lit up.

The evasive maneuvers had only made things worse. By the time he recovered, there was barely enough in the tanks to get home.

So no matter what he'd done, he would have had to leave.

He was still to blame for mismanaging his fuel.

Truth was, you could always blame yourself, because you were never perfect. And you were always afraid, somewhere, somehow. Fear was always in your stomach; it was a question of whether you let it control you.

It had that day. And every time he went for the bottle after that.

No more.

No, that wasn't true. He couldn't say that. What he could say was that it wasn't going to win today.

He could also say that he would come back, no matter what. He'd get back in the cockpit and head north again, feel the acid in his gut. And the next time the choice came between the prudent thing and the right thing, he would choose the right thing. Or try to.

Truth was, there were VC all over the place where Crush went down. The ridge was just the worst example. The flash Little Bear saw had more likely come from one of them than the Phantom's crew.

His real mistake wasn't the fuel or even leaving his friend. His real mistake was letting fear win later that night, and every night. That was his fuckup. It was something he knew, after all, but something he had to keep relearning.

"Repeat?"

It was Shotgun.

"Repeat what?" he said, barely remembering to key the mike.

"Did you say you're bingo fuel?"

He quick-glanced at his gauges—he had enough gas to get up to Turkey and back.

Well, almost.

"Negative." Skull pushed through his orbit, climbing back for another run at the line of trucks. He'd flown out nearly five miles; reorienting himself, he saw a distinct column of smoke rising from the highway. He could see no more flak.

"Waxed the antiair, but I think there's another truck or two at the end of the column," said Shotgun. "Bastards all look the same to me."

Skull saw Shotgun's A-10 above him. His wings were clean, except for the Sidewinders and ECM pod. It was all cannon-play from here on out.

"Let's dust these guys," Skull told him. "I don't want anything moving."

"My feeling exactly."

"You got your stereo on?"

"It's turned down."

"Well, crank it up," said Skull, pushing into his attack.

58

Shotgun leaned back and looked at the remains of the convoy, scattered in disarray on and along the road. No way those suckers were bothering anybody for a long, long time. He pushed the Hog to continue its climb into what was now a crowded sky—a pair of F-15's had screamed overhead, chasing the MiGs off far to the north, while a four-ship of F-16's had pulled into the neighborhood to see if they could join in the fun. Behind them two big, dark-colored grass-hoppers—big ol' MH-53J Pave Lows—were skimming toward the spot where they'd located Mongoose. Alongside them came an A-10A from another squadron, one of the SAR team's guardian angels.

Fuckin' Goose. He'd laid out half the stinking Iraqi army and was just hanging out having a smoke, right? Or just about. Because damn straight the guy waving down there was Mongoose, no way it was anybody else, and may-be Shotgun was at a thousand feet and moving over three hundred knots, but his eyes were still sharp as hell and no way, absolutely no way he could mistake his ol' section leader. There was a guy standing alone down there—

well, kneeling maybe—and it had to be Mongoose. Could only be.

Son of a bitch probably be flying tomorrow. Plus Shotgun was going to have to stand him a whole slew of drinks for letting him get waxed.

Only fair.

Probably have to throw in some Micky D bags too.

One thing he had to say—for a guy who hadn't sat in a Hog cockpit all that long, Knowlington had kicked butt. You could tell Skull liked to wallow in the mud the way he laughed at the flak on that last run, just went in and kissed it, got three stinking APCs and a truck on one run—not bad for a rookie.

Or an old coot, come to think of it.

Of course, he'd probably flown against those same guns in Viet Nam, and in something not nearly as good as a Hog. So he'd had practice.

"We're going back south and make sure their flank is clear," Skull told him. "I don't want nothing screwing us up now that we've worked up a sweat."

"I'm right behind you," said Shotgun.

He nudged his stick to get a slightly better angle off his wing, scanned his wedge of the world, and reached into his survival vest for his reserve cache of Good & Plenty. They weren't his favorite candy to eat while flying. The slick little torpedoes could shoot down your throat if you didn't pay attention, and then you lost all that flavor. But this was war and you had to take some chances.

59

He was played. He could feel the desert warming into daylight around him, felt the relentless approach of his enemy, but Mongoose could do nothing but stare upwards at the emptiness. He'd tried to stand, but got no further than his knees; he leaned back on them, wanting to collapse back but unable even to do that.

He no longer felt any pain. His consciousness was squeezed into a two-inch-by-two-inch rectangle, the space defined by his eyes, which saw only the blank sky.

When the Iraqis found him, they would shoot him. It was only fair.

He hadn't had a chance to read the letter. He regretted that. It was the only thing he regretted.

Maybe he would die before the soldiers found him. His knee was twisted and his arm broken. He was probably dehydrated beyond belief, and who knows what other injuries he had. He certainly didn't. All he knew was the blank space above.

Blank space filling with a dark angel.

Death.

The earth roared at the end, he thought, just like he'd heard it would.

Someone shouted at him over the din.

The angel was asking his name.

"James Johnson," he said.

"Major, you just ease back now, sir; we want to hop you into a stretcher just as a precaution. We got all the time in the world. Your colonel's blasted the shit out of half the Iraqi army," said the para-rescueman, squatting with him and helping him move his legs into a sitting position. "We'll have you home faster than you can say, 'Kiss my ass, Saddam.'"

60

Skull heard the Pave Low pilot practically yahoo as he got the thumbs-up from the rescue crew. Mongoose was alive.

"Shit, yeah," he acknowledged.

Not precisely military, except that it was, totally.

"Shit, yeah," said Shotgun.

Knowlington checked the Hog's dials as he ran a lazy arc south past the two choppers. At spec and with plenty of gas. Damn, he loved this plane.

Two Super Jolly Greens squatted in the hardscrabble terrain, fetching his pilot and making sure the Iraqis were dead.

Big, beautifully ugly choppers, just like in Nam.

Except, they weren't. They might look the same from the distance, but they'd been rebuilt from the ground up—stronger, meaner, much more capable.

More considered. More deliberate. Living by intelligence, not sheer brute force or instinct.

The facts were just the facts, back there, obscured by memory and smoke, fog of war and all that bullshit. It didn't change or get negated by the present; it stayed back there.

You had to deal with the present. It wasn't fair to blame

his drinking on that ride over Laos. He'd been drinking before that. Laos was what it was—a bad day with bad decisions and some luck for him, not for his buddy. It was back there now, squashed with the remains of bridges and guns and MiGs and APCs he'd wrecked or managed to evade. He had to deal with what was in front of him in the windscreen.

Fact was, he still wanted a drink. Fact was, the sting of whiskey in his throat would feel great.

But he wasn't going to taste it. Not today. Today he was going to struggle against it and find a lot to do at the base.

It'd be hard, though.

Knowlington checked his instruments again. He was just a mediocre pilot now, compared to most of the others in the squadron. Hell, this was going to look damn good, but the reality was it had been a turkey shoot; poor slobs had only one AAA gun, and they hadn't even set it up right.

More time in the cockpit wouldn't help. His reflexes were slower. And his eyes, his eyes were just normal eyes now.

Probably still had his share of luck, though. Must, to have gotten the chance to get back up here.

The thing was, he'd traded some of his flying ability for something else. He'd figured out where Mongoose was, walked his head through it like a commander should. He didn't have to prove himself in the cockpit anymore; that wasn't his job. His job was to get these guys up here.

And back.

"Hey, we got a knot of soldiers down here near those trees," radioed Shotgun over the squadron frequency as the two planes passed the area. "Kinda huddled down like maybe I won't see them."

"What are they doing?"

"Beats me. Maybe they're having breakfast. Shit, they're waving."

"Waving?"

"Yeah. What do you think?"

Knowlington began circling back. He gave the plane a smidgen of rudder as he settled on a precise line to the trees.

They were waving, all right. And they made a show of tossing away their guns.

"They want to surrender," Knowlington told Shotgun.

"Hot damn. Hog-tied prisoners. That's what I'm talking about. You cannot do this in any other plane. You ever see anybody surrender to an F-16? I don't think so. F-15? Ha, there's a joke."

Skull suppressed a laugh. But sure as hell, those soldiers did want to surrender.

"I accept your surrender in the name of the President of the United States, the commander in chief, and Kevin Karn," announced Shotgun.

"Who's Keven Karn?" Skull asked.

"My home-room teacher in tenth grade. He said I ought to go into the Air Force."

"I don't know what we're going to do with these guys," Knowlington told him. "It's a hell of a long walk back."

"Hell, stash them in one of the choppers. If they can't take 'em, I'll land and lash 'em onto the wings," said Shotgun.

I'll bet you will, Skull thought. "Stand by while I talk to the Pave Low."

61

Dixon jumped from the helicopter into a whirl of dust and sand, running behind one of the soldiers. He'd meant to stay aboard, but something about the adrenaline of the others pushed him out.

The one thing he hoped was that he didn't need to use his gun. Because sure as shit, then he was going to fuck up.

No one was firing, though. He ran forward a few steps, then stopped as he caught the silhouette of a Hog low and slow to the south. He turned and saw a second Pave Low landing about fifteen yards south of the chopper he'd just left; one of the commandos on the ground was waving its team out to help secure the area.

He turned back and saw the men from his Pave Low huddled around a man kneeling ahead.

Major Johnson.

He ran forward, the gun almost slipping from his hands. He slid onto his knees and stopped right at Johnson's chest.

"Mongoose, it's Dixon. Hey, Major, you okay?"

Mongoose groaned.

"Got a broken arm," said the sergeant. "Not sure what else. We're putting him on a stretcher."

Dixon nodded, leaned back over Johnson. "You're gonna be okay, Major."

Johnson blinked his eyes. Dixon looked him over, saw him move his feet. One of the para-rescuemen came up with a med kit; Dixon stepped back and let the man do his job.

"Looks like he shot that guy there," said the sergeant. He pointed to an Iraqi. "Maybe the rest of them too. Your Hogs must've smoked the trucks."

"No shit."

"Yeah. You fucking Hog drivers. Jesus, you guys want to win the whole war by yourselves, don't you?"

Dixon stood back and watched the Special Ops troops secure the area, checking over the dead Iraqis. He trotted over to the truck; he'd never seen the damage an A-10A could do to an enemy before.

The vehicle looked as if it had been ripped in two by a school of metal-eating sharks.

"Hey, you Lieutenant Dixon?" asked one of the helicopter crewmen, running up to him. "Major needs you to take care of something."

"I'm Dixon."

The soldier pointed toward the road. "Your guys captured a squad of Iraqis. You have to accept their surrender."

"What?"

"'Cause you're an officer and part of their squadron. Major Greer says the pilots want to make sure the Air Force gets full credit. Don't sweat it, these guys'll go with you."

Dixon looked over to the highway, thinking that Greer had somehow arranged a practical joke.

Six unarmed Iraqi soldiers, each fluttering a piece of white cloth above their heads, approached slowly, major smiles on their faces. A pair of Hogs crisscrossed above them, wagging their wings.

"Fucking Hogs," said the sergeant, sidling up next to Dixon as the Iraqis came forward. "What the hell are you guys going to do next?"

HOMEWARD
BOUND

62

In the rush that followed his return to base, Mongoose didn't have a chance to read the letter. He didn't have a chance to do anything besides drink water, have his arm fixed, and talk to people.

Talk to people mostly. First there were the official debriefers, including a pair of colonels from General Schwarzkopf's staff who were anxious to find out everything they could about the soldiers he'd encountered. There were so many Air Force people he lost track of who he was telling what to, and he even gave a short and undoubtedly uninformative debrief to a pair of British colonels wondering about the Roland.

Then there were the squadron personnel, and what seemed like every other member of the A-10A community, officers and enlisted, and maybe a few civilians thrown in for good measure. A lot of people, pilots especially, wanted to touch him for good luck.

Not that they were superstitious or anything.

Finally, there were the media, which treated him with more reverence than a four-year-old having a private audience with Santa Claus.

All of which confused the hell out of him because, after all, he had been shot down. And by his standards, that meant he'd screwed up.

No one else seemed to see it that way, though, and Mongoose was smart enough to keep his mouth shut and not contradict them. He remembered to take his aspirin, and had his arm cast signed so much it looked like an ink pad. And finally he found himself sitting alone in Colonel Knowlington's office, waiting for the colonel to return from some last-minute detail over at the host squadron commander's office.

So finally he reached in his pocket for Kathy's letter.

He found the crinkled photograph that had belonged to the Iraqi major first. He pulled it out and stared at it, a token that what he had gone through really had happened; it wasn't part of a surreal dream.

The strangers looked out from their glossy space with unknowing smiles. He ran his finger over the surface of the photograph before returning it to his pocket and retrieving the letter from home. It was crinkled and folded all to hell, and the inked address with his name had smeared and faded. He held it in the fist of his bad hand and slipped his finger under the flap to slit it open.

He stopped halfway.

What if, after all this, it had bad news? What if the one thing that had gotten him home turned out to be a Dear John letter, or worse?

Couldn't be. Would never be.

He drew his finger through.

> *Honey:*
> *Well, nothing much happened today. Again. Just a boring day.*
> *Robby's getting bigger by the minute. He misses you. I show him your picture every day. I tell him you're thinking about him and doing an important job for us all and that you'll be back soon.*
> *This morning we saw a pair of hawks circling in Felice's yard. I took him outside to see. "Pretty birds," I said. They swept down and we ran over to*

see, even though I didn't have our coats on. It's been warm.

Then I realized what they were doing. There was a little chipmunk on the ground and they killed it. I took Robby quick and ran inside. I don't think he saw.

They were so beautiful and mean at the same time. But of course they were just doing what they had to do.

We miss you so much—

"Am I interrupting you?"

Mongoose was so startled, he jumped to his feet.

"Hey, relax, Goose," said Knowlington, folding his arms. "Nobody's going to be shooting at you for quite a while."

"Sorry."

"That leg's okay?"

"Got a mile's worth of bandage on it. Feels okay. My arm's another story."

"You want me to open that for you?" asked Knowlington, pointing to the letter.

"No, no, it's fine." He refolded the envelope and slipped it back into his pocket.

"I wish I could say you don't look the worse for wear."

"I feel fine."

"I know that lie."

"I'd like to stay here with the squadron. Obviously I can't fly for a while, but I think I can put myself to pretty good use."

"You don't want to go back to see your wife and kid?"

"Well . . ." Mongoose couldn't think of anything to say. Or rather, he couldn't pick out just one thing.

"I'm sorry," he said finally.

"Sorry? For getting shot down?"

"No, for misjudging you," said Mongoose "I wasn't the easiest guy to get alone with at first, I realize that. I was wrong."

"If I had a complaint, I would have told you."

"Thanks for rescuing me."

"Aw, hell, I didn't rescue you. You thank Shotgun and the Special Ops guys."

"Shotgun told me you came up with the Mavericks and you ran the mission yourself. I appreciate that. I did misjudge you, Colonel," he added. "I thought, uh—"

"That I was a drunk? Yeah, well, maybe you had it right. I am. A sober one, though."

There was too much there for either one of them to talk about it directly. It didn't need words, though; they understood each other a lot better today than yesterday.

"Come on, I got a surprise for you," said Knowlington, jumping up.

"Surprise?"

"Yeah. Don't worry, it's not a party or anything, and I promise, no more generals or guys with cameras and dumb questions. But I had a little trouble figuring out how to get it set up, so you have to come down the hall with me."

Mongoose followed the colonel past Cineplex and the rest of the squadron rooms, down to an office belonging to the intelligence section that was housed in the back end of the Hog Heaven trailer complex. One of the intel officers was on the phone.

"Here you go," said the officer, handing him the phone. "All ready for you."

Mongoose took it warily. "Hello?"

"Jimmy? Are you okay?"

"Kath? Kath."

"I'm so glad you're okay."

"So am I," he said, and he slipped down into the chair, and in the background he heard little Robby crying. He glanced upward, and saw that Knowlington and the intel officer had left him alone, shutting the door so no one in the world would see that, in certain very special circumstances, Hog drivers did cry.

A Note to Readers

While this story is based on actual A-10A missions during the Gulf War, it is a work of fiction and should be treated as such. With the exception of historical figures, all characters and call signs in this book are invented and not based on actual individuals. While the bases and commands (other than the Devil Squadron) actually existed, they have been completely rearranged and reconstructed. Liberties have been taken in the name of dishing out an entertaining yarn.

Some details regarding operations and rescue procedures that could conceivably be of use to an enemy during combat have been omitted or obscured. They have not affected the telling of the tale.

The heroism and exploits of the characters in this book are but pale shadows of that displayed by the men and women who actually served during the Gulf War.

RESURRECTION DAY

A NOVEL

BRENDAN DUBOIS

PUTNAM

PENGUIN PUTNAM INC.
Online

Your Internet gateway to a virtual environment with
hundreds of entertaining and enlightening books from
Penguin Putnam Inc.

*While you're there, get the latest buzz on
the best authors and books around—*

Tom Clancy, Patricia Cornwell, W.E.B. Griffin,
Nora Roberts, William Gibson, Robin Cook,
Brian Jacques, Catherine Coulter, Stephen King,
Jacquelyn Mitchard, and many more!

**Penguin Putnam Online is located at
http://www.penguinputnam.com**

PENGUIN PUTNAM NEWS

Every month you'll get an inside look at our upcoming
books and new features on our site. This is an ongoing
effort to provide you with the most up-to-date
information about our books and authors.

**Subscribe to Penguin Putnam News at
http://www.penguinputnam.com/ClubPPI**